Jenna

Jenna

An Outback Brides of Wirralong Romance

Barbara Hannay

TULE
PUBLISHING

Chapter One

J ENNA MATTHEWS EMERGED from the bridal boutique's change cubicle in a halter-neck, crepe de Chine gown of palest mint, with her phone buzzing in her hand.

'Oh, you look absolutely gorgeous!' Cate, Jenna's best friend, who was also the bride-to-be, beamed at her. 'I love that dress on you. I think we've found the perfect—' Cate stopped in mid-gush as Jenna held up the phone.

'Sorry.' Jenna grimaced. 'Just need a moment to take an important call.'

Cate's grin vanished. 'Can't it wait five minutes?'

No, not really, Jenna wanted to reply. The client was from the top rung of Melbourne's financial circles and she'd been thrilled to land his case. After years of slogging away in highly competitive corporate law, she'd finally reached the point where she was trusted with major clients. That achievement, however, meant being on call, virtually twenty-four-seven.

Normally, Jenna didn't mind these demands, but right now she also remembered that Cate had tried three times to book a date to find a bridesmaid's dress and there were limits to a girlfriend's patience. And the boutique's sales assistant was shooting her daggers as well.

Lifting a hand to momentarily placate them, Jenna spoke into her phone. 'Simon, I'm sorry. I'm—in a meeting right now. Can I call you back? Say around seven this evening?'

Luckily, this was acceptable, although the concession was made grudgingly. Okay. With that settled, Jenna figured a seven o'clock deadline should give her plenty of time to shop with Cate, as well as enjoying the mandatory drink at their favourite bar, while Cate filled her in on details of the wedding.

Jenna could then work until eleven or so, which wasn't unusual for her. Working late gave her quite a buzz, actually, not unlike the buzz of facing each day with a mountain of new files on her desk. It was all about meeting the challenge.

Still, these things could be overdone.

Ending the call, she turned to Cate and the sales assistant, who were, she was pleased to note, all smiles again. 'This dress feels great,' she told them, honestly. She really loved the swish of the skirt as she moved and the way the lining skimmed silkily against her body.

'It looks fab,' enthused Cate. 'That pale mint colour really suits you and it'll be perfect for a country wedding.'

'A *country* wedding?' Jenna couldn't quite hide her shock.

'Well, yes, of course.' Cate gave a helpless shake of her head. 'You can't have forgotten, Jen. You know the wedding's in Wirralong.'

'Oh, yes, of course,' Jenna quickly covered, hoping she hadn't caused even more distress for Cate. 'Sorry. Momentary lapse.' Except that she hadn't known this at all, or if she had been told, she'd somehow forgotten. How could she have overlooked such an important detail?

Jenna knew, of course, that Cate and her fiancé had both grown up in the Wirralong district in rural Victoria. She also knew they'd met up again in their home town six months ago and their romance had been a whirlwind affair. But despite Cate's country roots and her plans to spend her married life buried back in the bush, Cate had also spent a decade working in Melbourne.

Jenna had met her when they were both newbies in the firm, fresh out of uni—Cate as an accountant and Jenna as an intern. They'd even shared a flat in those early years, embracing the café and clubbing scene with regular enthusiasm.

Jenna had assumed her friend was still as enamoured as she was with everything the city had to offer. For heaven's sake, Melbourne provided a veritable host of absolutely brilliant wedding venues. And they were all so wonderfully convenient.

Unfortunately, this matter of convenience was yet another stumbling block for Jenna. Of course, she'd known that the wedding would take up an entire Saturday, but that was fine. While she worked most weekends, she would happily give a full day to her girlfriend, taking Cate out for breakfast before the necessary hairdressing and makeup appointments.

But a trip into the country was another matter entirely. Almost certainly, Jenna would need to drive out to Wirralong on Friday afternoon and she wouldn't be back till late Sunday.

Her problem wasn't just the huge time suck. Jenna didn't *do* country. Not ever.

Not anymore.

When had she not been paying attention?

This was her mistake, though, and it was way too late to question or complain about the plans. Jenna certainly wouldn't let her good friend down. She would have to view this wedding as yet another challenge, albeit a much more personal challenge than corporate law, but one worthy of her best effort.

Resolute as she turned to the full-length mirror, Jenna took a closer look at her reflection. Wow. The dress really was amazing, and Cate was right—it suited her perfectly. The halter-neck showed off her shoulders, which were possibly her best asset and it was ages since she'd worn such a softly flowing, feminine skirt.

Jenna's usual apparel consisted of dark suits (mostly black—this was Melbourne, after all) and silk shirts in white, cream or grey. These she combined with the highest heels she could manage, a necessity required by the gap between her average height and the lofty heights of the men who filled her working life.

It was a bit of a shock now to see herself looking so undeniably feminine.

'We'll need to take the hemline up a little,' the sales assistant was saying as she whipped a tape measure from around her neck. 'But that's not a problem. We have an in-house dressmaker who can deal with that in a flash.'

'Excellent,' Cate responded with a beaming smile. 'So, are you happy with this dress, Jen?'

Jenna glanced again at her reflection, imagining her hair released from its usual neat updo and a bouquet of blossoms in her arms. She would be almost unrecognisable and, for some reason she couldn't quite explain, that possibility appealed. 'Yes, I am,' she said. 'Very happy.'

'Great.' Cate clapped her hands, clearly delighted and no doubt relieved to have another wedding detail locked in.

AT LAST IT was sundown, bringing the first hint of a cool breeze. Steaks and onions sizzled on the barbecue and iceboxes were filled with cold champers and beer. Sam Twist rolled his shoulders, easing out the tension that had plagued him too often during these past hot, dry months.

Determined to relax this evening, he turned his back on the vista of bleached paddocks stretching to the horizon. Raising his beer, he sent a smile to his friends, who were gathered on the last remaining patch of green lawn in front of his homestead.

Seated in canvas chairs, happily chatting, or gathered around the barbecue and flipping steaks, everyone looked at ease and light-hearted. And tonight, like them, Sam also refused to stress about the drought that held their properties in its deadly grip. Tonight was about Cate and Craig, two of his oldest friends, reaching back to their primary school days, and Sam was hosting their pre-wedding gathering.

With the bucks party safely behind them and the wedding just a week away, this evening's do was a casual, low-key affair for the wedding party and a few of the bride and groom's closest mates. A chance for the main players to meet, mingle and chill out before the big day.

Sam was to be Craig's best man and this evening he was looking forward to meeting the bridesmaid who would be his partner. Jenna Matthews was her name. But her name and the fact that she was single were all Sam knew about her. She wasn't from around these parts.

'So,' Sam said, as he topped up Cate's wine glass with suitably chilled bubbly. 'I take it your bridesmaid's not here yet. She's driving from Melbourne, isn't she? Hope she hasn't got herself lost.'

Cate's grimace was clearly apologetic. 'Sorry, Sam. I thought Craig had already warned you. Jenna can't make it this evening. I'm afraid she's too busy.'

'No kidding?' Just in time, Sam edited the skepticism

from his voice. He didn't want to upset Cate. But, seriously? *Too busy* seemed a pretty lame excuse for a bridesmaid. It wasn't as if there'd been a host of these pre-wedding commitments. And wasn't she supposed to be Cate's best friend?

The fact that Sam had been looking forward to meeting the woman was irrelevant. Sure, his social life could benefit from an injection of new blood, and the prospect of a casual meeting with said bridesmaid before the formalities of the wedding had been a welcome one. But his social life wasn't the issue here. A best friend and bridesmaid made a few sacrifices, surely?

Cate gave a shrug. 'You've no idea what it's like for a corporate lawyer. Jenna's schedule is beyond crazy.'

'She's a corporate lawyer?'

'Yes.' Cate rolled her eyes. 'Hasn't Craig told you anything?'

'He was kinda distracted last time we spoke.'

'Distracted by the stripper at the bucks' party, I suppose.'

Sam wisely ignored this and Cate wisely didn't push. 'As I remember,' he said, 'the topics under discussion were wool prices and the level of water in our dams.'

'Well, yes, I can imagine.' Cate sobered momentarily, but she was probably as reluctant as anyone else at this gathering to dwell on that topic tonight, and she brightened quite quickly. 'Anyway, Jenna works at the same firm I've worked at for the past ten years. We both started there straight out of uni.'

'And now you've escaped,' Sam said with a grin.

'Indeed I have. I finished up yesterday.' With a rueful smile, Cate tapped her wineglass. 'I'm sure I don't really need any more of this, after last night's farewell.'

'I hope your bridesmaid managed to get to that party?' Sam said. *Just checking.*

'Yes. For an hour or so.'

An hour or so. Fun girl. He ignored the slug of disappointment as he mentally crossed off Jenna Matthews as a potential source of interest. A workaholic corporate lawyer wasn't even remotely his type.

'So now you won't be able to meet Jenna till the actual wedding,' Cate said.

He gave an offhand shrug. 'I guess I'll cope.'

Cate, however, was watching him with an unsettling degree of interest. A hint of mild amusement gleamed in her light blue eyes. 'Poor Sam,' she said. 'I take it you're between transferees?'

He pretended to be offended. 'That's a bit harsh.' He knew Cate was referring to his preference for dating women who'd been transferred into town.

Rather than choosing companions from the small pool of local girls, Sam tended to enjoy the company of women who worked in Wirralong's medical centre, or in real estate, or banking. Entertaining for a while, they would eventually move on, leaving him free to explore fresh horizons.

And no, he'd never stopped to examine the reasons for

this preference too closely.

'Pretty sunset,' Cate said, turning to the west where the sun was spreading a blaze of fire above the almost bare paddocks. 'Wonder if it means rain?'

'I doubt it.'

'As long as it doesn't rain next weekend.'

Thanks to drought-induced austerity measures, the wedding would *not* be held at the district's most successful and popular venue, Wirra Station, but at Longholme, the sheep property that had been in Craig's family for four generations. An unpretentious outdoor affair was planned, with tables set under marquees, and Craig's mother, Louise, who'd spent a lifetime cooking for family and shearers alike, apparently in her element as chief caterer.

Sam cast another glance at the cloudless sky. 'I'm sure you're safe. It's not going to rain on your wedding day.' Under his breath, he added, 'Unfortunately.'

Chapter Two

'So, tell me about the best man.'

'Well, he's Craig's oldest friend and his name's Sam Twist.'

'Yes, I know that much. Sam Twist sounds like a pirate.'

Cate laughed. 'Sam's not a pirate, exactly. He runs sheep, but if you swapped his akubra for a bandana and earring, I suppose he might look the part. He does have a somewhat dangerous vibe.'

Interesting. Jenna hadn't given her partner at this wedding much thought until now, when she was actually in Wirralong. With the wedding just a day away, she and Cate were both staying in a hotel in town, sparing Cate's widowed father the hassle of hosting them out on his farm.

Jenna had shouted Cate dinner and there'd been champagne involved—it had seemed appropriate and Cate hadn't objected—and after the meal the girls retired to the old-fashioned, comfy lounge to linger over the last of their wine.

'Is Sam married?' Jenna asked.

'Gosh, no. He's a bit of a player, I'm afraid. It will take someone *very* special to pin him down.'

'A challenge then.' Too late, Jenna realised that she'd probably drunk too much bubbly. 'Sorry, scratch that,' she amended quickly. 'That was the champers talking. I am *not* in any way, shape or form, remotely interested in pinning down a country boy.'

'Oh, go on,' Cate teased. 'You'd make a great country wife.'

'Ha, ha.'

'Just think. We could truly stay best friends forever.'

'And enter baking competitions together?' Jenna rolled her eyes to the ceiling. 'Sorry. You might as well just shoot me now.'

Cate gave a smiling shake of her head. 'It's not so bad out here, when you give it a chance.'

'I'm sure it's not.' Jenna hastily backpedaled. 'I'm not dissing your lifestyle choice, Cate. And anyway, you grew up here, so you know exactly what you're in for.' As Jenna said this, she quickly censored memories of the property in outback Queensland where she'd grown up. 'I think you'll be a perfect country woman. It's just not my scene.'

'I was quite sure it wasn't my scene either, till I caught up with Craig again.'

Jenna watched her friend blush, saw her happy, swoony smile and felt a stab of envy. It must feel damn wonderful to be so happily certain about a man, but Jenna couldn't imagine ever letting herself go to the point where she fell head over heels. Caution was her watchword.

'You've found the perfect man and that makes all the difference, of course,' she said gently.

'I know. I've spent the past ten years partying hard in Melbourne and Craig was here all the time. It's crazy, really, to think of the guys I've dated over the past decade and now I'm marrying the boy who threw burrs in my hair in fifth grade.'

'He was trying to get your attention, of course. He probably fancied you even back then.'

Cate dimpled. 'Yeah, apparently he did.'

'That's so sweet.' Jenna blinked, hoping to hide the sudden dampness in her eyes. 'You've given me genuine goose bumps.'

Waving her now empty champagne flute, as if it was a magic wand, Cate said, 'It'll be your turn next. I just know there's a perfect man somewhere out there, just waiting for you, Jen.'

'Hmmm.' Problem was, even if Jenna actually found him, she very much doubted she would take the plunge.

WIRRALONG WAS UNDENIABLY beautiful, as country towns went. Despite an obvious lack of rain that had drained the countryside of colour, Jenna liked the way the town nestled into the landscape.

Without towering skyscrapers or sprawling new suburbs,

the place had a romantic, old-fashioned vibe. And yet, despite the heritage buildings and vintage shop fronts, the World War One memorial and other echoes from the past, Wirralong was quite busy on a Saturday morning and the essential services were totally up to speed. The sunny café where Jenna and Cate breakfasted served perfect coffee and smashed avocado on sourdough.

So different from the dusty, isolated town in western Queensland that Jenna had left when she was ten and had been trying to forget ever since. Now, it seemed she might be able to enjoy a weekend in the country after all, which was a relief.

She had even, bravely, turned off her phone. Didn't they say there was a first time for everything?

And so, a pleasant leisurely morning merged into a relaxed afternoon, although an undeniable buzz of excitement simmered as the friendly girls at the Hair Affair salon set to work on styling Jenna and Cate's hair and painting their nails.

'And how are you going to have your hair?' the smiling hairdresser, Elsa, asked Jenna. 'Up or down?'

'Up,' said Jenna.

'Down,' said Cate from the chair beside her. 'Come on, Jenna, loosen up for once.'

Their gazes met in the long mirror in front of them and Jenna wondered if it was the talk of the pirate last night that had prompted her to take the safe route. At work, she habitually wore her hair up these days, using a straightener and hairspray to eliminate any tendency to curl, keeping the look neat, no-nonsense and businesslike. But now she caught the glint of challenge in her friend's blue eyes.

'Down would be fine,' she said. This was Cate's day, after all.

BY THE TIME the girls arrived back at the hotel, wonderfully transformed by Elsa and Serenity's brilliant ministrations, their bouquets had arrived, delivered by an equally talented florist. The flowers looked and smelled divine—creamy lilies and pink rosebuds for Jenna, and a slightly larger and more elaborate version with white roses and baby's breath for Cate. And then it was finally time for Jenna to help Cate into her dress.

Cate looked beautiful, of course, although she almost spoiled her makeup when she had a weepy moment thinking about her mum, who had passed away eighteen months earlier.

'I'm sure your mum's watching you and smiling with massive love and pride,' Jenna offered gently, along with tissues for careful dabbing. It seemed the right thing to say, even though Jenna rarely allowed herself to imagine that her own deceased father might be looking down from heaven.

Do not think about that now.

At least Cate was soon smiling again.

And the smiles grew broader when Cate's father and her young brothers, Dan and Tim, arrived in their suitably beribboned vintage cars, parking in specially reserved spots right in front of the hotel.

'Aren't you two a sight for sore eyes?' exclaimed Cate's father, clearly gobsmacked by his daughter's transformation, while Dan and Tim grinned shyly.

A small crowd had gathered on the footpath by this time and, as Cate, Jenna and the men emerged from the hotel, there was much grinning, waving and cheering, plus cries of 'Good luck' and 'God bless.'

Waving back to them as Tim helped her into the backseat of the smaller vintage vehicle, Jenna had to admit that certain aspects of country life, these friendly bystanders for example, were very heartwarming indeed.

THE WEDDING CEREMONY was to take place in a paddock at Longholme, beside the river, at a point where the banks were quite high and lined with gumtrees and willows. It was the hour before dusk, that peaceful time of day when purple shadows lengthened and the land was lit by a soft golden light.

A pretty setting, for sure, but Jenna couldn't quite believe Cate had taken the risk of an outdoor wedding, requiring a procession across an open paddock of dry crackling grass. She'd checked the internet and there was a perfectly acceptable wedding chapel for hire at Wirra Station, but Cate and Craig had been keen to economise, given the ongoing drought, which was fair enough. At least there didn't seem to be any threat of rain.

Rows of seats had been set up and were already filled with wedding guests, a string quartet was playing, and Jenna could see Craig and his best man standing in a flower-bedecked area at the front of the guests, with a woman, who was, presumably, the wedding celebrant.

And now, as Cate and her father emerged from their car, the music stopped and an expectant hush fell over everyone. All heads turned their way and, in that moment, it didn't matter where this wedding was held.

Jenna was acutely conscious that a time-honoured cere-mony was about to take place for two lovely people who would pledge to love each other forever. And damn it, as she thought about this, her throat was suddenly tight with emotion, her mouth pulling out of shape.

Don't you dare cry.

She was appalled by her sentimental weakness. Who ever heard of a blubbering bridesmaid? What had happened to her cool, shrewd, lawyer facade?

Somehow, thank heavens, she managed to collect herself and to send Cate and her father an encouraging smile. Then there was no time for wobbly moments, as the string quartet struck up the well-known opening bars of the wedding march. It was time to head off, preceding Cate down the makeshift aisle where a strip of carpet runner had been thoughtfully placed.

Remember to smile.

SO THIS WAS the lawyer?

Sam, standing beside Craig and looking back over his shoulder, stared with way too much interest at the bridesmaid who walked towards them. He wasn't sure what he'd been expecting, but certainly not a slender siren in a softly floating, pale dress that made him think of mermaids.

Was this really Jenna Matthews, the workaholic corporate lawyer? This girl with glossy, fair hair that curled and bounced around her lovely bare shoulders? This girl with beautiful sea-green eyes that seemed to hold secrets designed to keep a man guessing?

Sam was so distracted by the unexpectedness of this vision, he had to discipline himself to pay attention to the bride and her father.

Right. Okay. Cate looked lovely, of course, with the softly glowing beauty that seemed reserved for happy brides. And Ted, her father, couldn't have looked prouder.

But Sam couldn't help taking another good look at the bridesmaid. In that same moment, she looked his way and their gazes connected and he only just held it together as she focused her full siren-like attention on him.

WHOA.

Jenna was so distracted, she almost stumbled. Perhaps she could blame Cate for suggesting that Craig's best man was a pirate, but whatever the reason, she couldn't help staring. Which didn't really make sense. Most men looked great when they were standing straight and tall, in dark formal dinner suits complete with bow ties.

And yet, Jenna's attention was totally captured by the best man. The sheen of his dark hair, the breadth of his shoulders, the easy way he held himself. And that was before he had turned and his gaze caught hers.

For sure, only a pirate could rob a girl of breath at first sighting. Crazily, and without warning, Jenna had the whole weak-kneed, lightning-bolt attraction thing happening.

So unexpected. Jenna was quite thrown for a moment or two, until she reminded herself that she was no longer a naïve girl, but a confident, corporate player. She knew exactly how to handle alpha males and pirates. No question.

Chapter Three

'I BELIEVE THIS is our cue to dance.'

Jenna nodded and smiled. Took a deep breath. Throughout the reception, which was held under a giant marquee, she'd been ridiculously conscious of Sam, seated at the head table as she was, but separated from her by the bride and groom.

She'd been introduced to him, of course, a formality that had come sometime after their first unofficial meeting, when they'd been required to link arms and follow the happy bridal couple back down the aisle.

'G'day,' Sam had murmured then, as he'd tucked Jenna's hand into the crook of his elbow. 'You look beautiful.'

A predictable enough greeting she supposed, but when it was teamed with a sexy, rascally smile and an accompanying sparkle of light grey eyes, she'd almost forgotten her plan to be cool and in control.

Thankfully, she'd recovered somewhat during the taking of the photographs, which had involved a certain amount of standing around and waiting, while the photographer focused on Cate and Craig. She'd made sure that the conversation topics were safe and careful and, no doubt, boring for Sam. Basically, she'd focused on the weather and the success of the wedding. And perhaps he got the message. There'd certainly been no flirting.

Even so, Jenna had remained super-aware of him all evening, finding herself keen to catch a glimpse, an occasional smile, conscious of the easy asides he'd made during the meal, keeping the bride and groom entertained and relaxed, and keeping everyone in stitches when it was time for his best man's speech.

Now, the official photographs and the speeches were over and a very pleasant wedding feast had been enjoyed. Cate and Craig had completed their bridal waltz on the specially created timber dance floor and it was time for the best man and bridesmaid to join them. Which also meant it was time for Jenna to morph into Ice Princess mode. In the interests of self-preservation.

However, this idea, like many bright ideas, proved to be far easier in theory than in practice.

Proximity had a power all of its own, Jenna soon discovered. Stepping close to Sam Twist, taking his hand in hers and allowing his other hand to settle at the small of her back was quite a dangerous process in reality. Dangerously enjoyable.

It was ages since Jenna had been out dancing, even longer since she'd waltzed with a handsome man, and she'd almost forgotten the pleasure involved. The surprising allure of finding herself held close to a smooth, manly suit and a crisp white shirt. The brush of her cheek against a tanned, muscular throat. The illusive but enticing hint of aftershave.

Not to mention the strong, assured masculine body, at one with hers, guiding her expertly, but ever so subtly.

Sam Twist was a confident and skilful dancer. Jenna suspected he would be confident and capable with most things he undertook.

Don't think about sex with him. Are you crazy, girl?

'Are you enjoying yourself?' he asked, as he whisked her around the dance floor.

'Tonight's been wonderful,' she said. 'Just the loveliest wedding.'

'Unpretentious.'

'Yes. Perhaps that's why I've enjoyed it so much.'

Sam smiled.

'You seem surprised?' she suggested.

'I am, yes.'

'I know. I've surprised myself.' And yet it was the truth. Jenna had thoroughly enjoyed the delicious, home-cooked food, the simple speeches laced with love and good humour. Even more surprising, though, she'd actually enjoyed the outdoor setting and the knowledge that sheep paddocks and vineyards stretched into the night in all directions beyond the brightly lit marquee. Weird, when she normally took comfort from massive tower blocks and bustling city streets.

Sam slowed their pace now, as other guests joined them

on the dance floor, and he steered Jenna towards the outer edge of the crowd.

'So, what have you particularly enjoyed about this evening?' he asked.

She laughed to cover the shock of her first thought—that *he* had been a definite bonus. 'It might be as simple as the fact that I've turned off my phone,' she confessed.

'Ah. Wise woman.' He sounded amused. 'But you know phone deprivation can be serious. You might need counselling.'

'Almost certainly.' Jenna laughed again—when had she last laughed like this?

Of course, there'd been times tonight when her fingers had itched to reach for the phone she'd stowed in her evening bag. She'd staunchly resisted, however, and had eventually decided that ignoring the damn thing might even be liberating.

By now, Sam had stopped dancing and they were standing on the grass at the edge of the marquee. 'Can I tell you something?' he asked.

'Sure,' she responded, perhaps incautiously.

'I meant it when I said you're beautiful.'

'Oh.' An inadequate response, but all she could think of.

Taking her hands lightly in his, he looked clear into her eyes and smiled. 'Forgive me, Jenna Matthews, but you'll be leaving in the morning, and we don't have much time. I wanted you to know that you're not just beautiful, you're utterly bewitching.'

Jenna was quite stunned into silence. Sam was, most definitely, hitting on her now and a sensible woman would back away. The man was a pirate after all, and to remain close and smiling could be as dangerous as walking the plank.

And yet, she was attracted—oh, my gosh yes—attracted to those damn sparkling eyes and to the tanned rugged body that his suit couldn't disguise. If any bewitching had occurred this evening, she suspected that she'd been the victim.

Moments ago, while she'd been dancing just a little too close, experiencing breathtaking brushes of his body with hers, she'd thought of little else but getting naked with him.

Despite Sam's openness, though, she wasn't going to make any such confession.

Then again … as he'd said … she was leaving in the morning. And Cate had more or less implied that this man was a perennial bachelor. In other words, he wasn't just the most attractive man Jenna had met in ages, possibly in living memory, he was perfect for a fling.

And given how hard she'd been working, perhaps she'd earned a little fun.

Jenna looked to the dancers. The playlist had moved on to Seal's 'Kiss from a Rose' and Craig was now twirling his mum around the floor, while Cate was dancing with her father. Cate was also looking over her dad's shoulder to Jenna, watching her with such a knowing smile she might just as well have called out 'Go get him'.

Jenna knew she was blushing.

'Can I get you a drink?' Sam asked. 'Or would you like to keep dancing?'

'Perhaps a drink.' She needed a little breathing space, time to collect her thoughts, to rein in her galloping libido. This was a sedate country wedding, after all, a family affair with aunts and uncles, cousins and kids. Even if they'd wanted to, she and Sam couldn't just race off into the night.

He sat beside her, bringing a bottle from the ice bucket to top up their glasses. She wondered what they would talk about and decided to play it safe by leading the way.

'I loved your speech,' she told him. 'It's great that you've known Craig since the first day of primary school. You obviously had so many funny stories to share.'

'And I only told the safest ones,' Sam said with a wink.

'It must be great to have friends who reach so far back.' She hadn't stayed in touch with anyone from her childhood.

'Cate was a year behind us,' said Sam.

'And Craig threw burrs in her hair in fifth grade.'

'Is that what she told you?' He chuckled. 'I missed that tender moment. Pity. I could have shared that with everyone, too.'

They were both smiling as they looked towards the dance floor. Cate and Craig were back in each other's arms.

'Great couple,' Sam said.

'Really great, yes.'

'Marriage suits them.'

'Mmmm.' Jenna knew Sam was watching her now, but she kept her gaze on the dancers, sure that if she looked his way she would find herself trapped by that amused, teasing gaze.

'So you've always lived in Melbourne?' he asked.

'No, Brisbane for most of my schooling. Well, there was a little time before that in country Queensland.' Unwilling to go into details about that time, she quickly hurried on. 'I studied law at UQ and my mother and sister still live in Brisbane.'

'Snap,' said Sam. 'My mother's retired to the Sunshine Coast.'

'It's beautiful there.' Jenna wondered where Sam's father was, but she didn't like to ask. Such questions opened windows she preferred to leave closed. 'So she's left you to look after the sheep?'

He grinned. 'Indeed. While you're knee deep in corporate law.'

'More like up to my neck.'

His smile dimmed as he acknowledged this with a thoughtful nod. 'So it's demanding work?'

'A-huh. Especially for a woman.'

'Breaking into the boys' club?'

Jenna was impressed by the nuance of sympathy in Sam's voice. Perhaps he was a very good actor? Even so, it made a change to meet a man who feigned interest and didn't just want to talk about himself.

An interesting mix, this Sam Twist. A few minutes ago she'd been ready to race away with him and tear his clothes off, and now they were on the brink of a genuine conversation. Despite the attraction that simmered below the surface with a slow-burning heat, she sensed he was the kind of guy who would listen if she'd really wanted to pour her heart out.

'Corporate law is steeped in male privilege,' she said. 'So many cocky males, all desperate to compete, taking on extra work, claiming knowledge they don't necessarily have.'

'So how do women make their way past that?'

She shrugged. 'It's sink or swim really. Female lawyers are conditioned to believe they're imposters, not smart enough or not ready. I decided to look on the work as a challenge.'

Again, he looked thoughtful. 'A daily marathon?'

Jenna blinked. Was that what her life was like? Those piles of documents on her desk? The long hours? Marathon after marathon? 'Perhaps,' she said quietly.

'At least you're taking this weekend off.'

'Half of it, yes.' And she had to admit, she was enjoying the weirdness of the freedom intensely. Too much?

SAM THOUGHT THE reception might never end, but when he checked the time, he was surprised to find that it wasn't very late at all. The problem was his impatience. While dancing and chatting with Jenna was fine, more than fine in fact, he desperately wanted to whisk her away. Soon. Now.

No question. He needed her to himself.

The wanting was fierce, breathtakingly so. He'd never met a girl quite like this bridesmaid. Beautiful, yet tough. Sharp-witted, yet vulnerable. Sexy as hell.

'So tell me something non-lawyerly about yourself,' he said in a bid to curb his impatience.

Jenna shook her head. 'I'm sure it's time I asked *you* a few questions.'

'You don't want to know about farming and sheep.'

'I'm sure you have other talents.' It was hard to tell if she was flirting, but he couldn't quite catch her eye.

'And please don't ask me about climate change,' he added.

'No, Sam, I'll spare you that one.' Instead she asked, 'Do you live alone?'

'Mostly.'

This caught Jenna's attention. For a moment, as she sent him a quick searching glance, Sam thought she would quiz him further on this, but of course she was too clever to ask the obvious. Instead she said, 'So I guess you must be able to cook?'

'Just. I can manage a rather basic repertoire.'

'Me, too,' she admitted with a sheepish smile. 'I eat out way too often. And I work too many hours, so I can't ask you informed questions about books or movies. I hate to admit it, but I'm actually bloody boring.'

'I doubt that, Jenna.'

She chanced another glance his way and looked almost shy as if she'd read his thoughts—that she couldn't possibly be boring in bed.

'Ah,' she said suddenly, her face lighting with a burst of enthusiasm. 'I just got the signal from Cate. She and Craig are getting ready to leave.'

About time. 'Right.' Sam tried not to sound too eager, but he was encouraged that Jenna seemed to share the same restlessness that gripped him. But of course, more patience was required as Cate and Craig dutifully shared individual goodbyes with all of their guests, moving slowly around the circle, stopping for kisses and hugs.

Craig was all smiles when he reached Sam. 'Thanks for everything, mate,' he said as he gripped Sam's hand.

'No problem. It's been a great wedding, and I'm wishing all the very best for you and Cate.' Sam slapped Craig's shoulder. 'Have an ace honeymoon, won't you?'

Another grin from Craig. 'I'll do my best.'

And then Cate was there, slipping her arms around Sam and giving him a tight hug. 'Take care of my bestie,' she murmured in his ear.

'I plan to.'

Releasing him from the hug, Cate stood with her hands on his shoulders, looking him squarely in the eye. 'I mean it, Sam,' she said with quiet but surprising determination.

'Jenna's a special girl. Look after her.' He was glad Jenna was out of hearing.

'I will,' he said. 'Although she seems quite capable of looking after herself.'

Cate's eyes narrowed. 'Don't be too sure about that.' But then she was smiling and kissing his cheek, giving him a wink before moving on.

And Sam was left wondering. What the hell was that about?

JENNA HADN'T GIVEN a moment's thought to the bridal bouquet until Cate and Craig were about to get into their car, which Cate's brothers had decorated with masses of ribbons and balloons. The guests, primed with good wine and good cheer, were gathered close, waving, calling heartfelt wishes.

Craig opened the car door for his bride and she turned back for a final wave. In that same moment, she yelled, 'Here, Jenna, catch!' And the lovely arrangement of lilies and roses came sailing through the air in a perfect arc.

Jenna had only to hold out her arms and the flowers were hers.

'Hooray!' called the crowd.

No, no, she wanted to tell them. *I might have caught a bouquet, but it doesn't mean anything, really. Absolutely not.*

She had no plans to be the next girl to marry and settle down. This wasn't a moment for brutal honesty, however. And when she glanced towards Sam, she could see he was looking as disconcerted as she felt, which she found strangely comforting and yet unsettling. Yikes, her emotions were all over the place tonight.

But before she could dwell on that thought, Craig's car was taking off, amidst rousing cheers, disappearing down two well-worn dirt tracks and into the night. Jenna watched the floating balloons and red tail-lights until they disappeared, then she looked up at the sky, cloudless and boundless and black, glittering with stars.

Without warning, she was suddenly back in her childhood, in western Queensland, standing out in a paddock just like this one, looking up at the night sky with her father. Her father had his arm around her shoulders and she could feel the weight of it, warm and reassuring.

'No need to be scared, Jen. The night's just the same as the daytime with the lights turned out.'

In that moment Jenna had trusted him, totally, with the bone-deep love and trust of a little girl for her daddy.

Oh, Dad, why did you have to go and spoil it?

AN ARM CAME around Jenna's shoulders and she jumped.

It was Sam. 'Are you okay?' he asked.

'Yes, of course.' Squaring her shoulders, she pinned on a smile, banishing unwanted memories.

'Look,' he said next. 'This might sound crass, so I'd rather you didn't slap me in front of all these good folk. But I was wondering if you might like to come back to my place.' He spoke casually enough, but when she turned to look at him, she saw heat intense enough to burn.

Her response was just as fierce—a tug of desire so deep and low, she almost melted on the spot. She needed to take a breath before she could speak. 'I'd like that,' she said. After all, what better way to forget about the past than a lusty night with a pirate?

Chapter Four

S O, SHE'D SAID yes, and it was going to happen. She would spend the night with this man and tomorrow she would head back to Melbourne, having enjoyed a one-night stand with a gorgeous bachelor. Which was, Jenna had to admit, her preferred form of dating. Her working life left no room for longer relationships and the messy entanglements that so often came with them.

Just the same, she was conscious of a strange mix of nervousness and excitement as she and Sam finally left the party, driving off down the bumpy dirt track in his SUV. Perhaps he sensed this. With a flip of a switch on the dashboard there was music—soothing and innocuous piano— playing low.

'That's not too annoying?' he asked.

'No, it's fine. I like it.' The rippling piano was strangely comforting as she looked out at paddocks with sparse clumps of dried grass, turned to silver by the moonlight.

Rounding a final bend before the track met the main road, they passed an owl sitting on a fence post. As the car's headlights swept over the scene, the owl took off, silver wings flapping gracefully.

'I suppose he's hoping to catch a mouse,' Jenna suggested.

'I'd say so.'

'But there won't be many mice about, will there? Not when the country's so dry?'

'Probably not.' Sam turned to her with another of his amused smiles. 'That's a rather interesting observation from a dyed-in-the-wool city woman.'

Jenna decided not to remind him that she'd spent a good chunk of her childhood in the outback. 'Even a city woman who's widely read?' she countered.

'Touché,' he responded with a chuckle.

He drove on, tyres spinning smoothly over bitumen now. Leaning back in the car seat, Jenna tried to relax, which wasn't easy given that she'd been propositioned by six feet of ultra-sexy male who now sat mere inches away.

It did occur to her that driving off into the bush with a man she'd just met might not be the wisest thing she'd ever done, that perhaps she should have at least suggested they go back to her hotel. But Sam Twist was Craig's oldest friend, the good mate he'd chosen as his best man, and despite her own jokes about his piratical tendencies, she hadn't sensed anything dodgy about him.

In fact her instincts had picked up a genuinely okay vibe. And, anyway, she was curious about his home.

So now her thoughts kept racing ahead, imagining their

arrival at Sam's house. One moment she was picturing them having a sedate nightcap, on a homestead verandah perhaps, or on his sofa. The next, her imagination went wild and they were tearing each other's clothes off.

'How long will it take to reach your place?' she asked in a bid to remain calm.

'About fifteen minutes.'

She fiddled with the clasp of her evening bag. Fifteen minutes was plenty of time to retrieve her phone and check the many messages that would be piling up, some of which were bound to be important.

'Don't,' said Sam.

'Don't what?'

'Don't check your phone.'

'What makes you think I was going to?'

In the faint glow of the dashboard she saw his face crease with yet another slow smile. 'Masculine intuition.'

Smart arse. Jenna almost grabbed the phone just to put him in his place. Except ... if she was honest, she didn't really want to download that inevitable raft of messages. She couldn't remember the last time she'd been so reckless as to ignore her phone, but she was relishing the delicious freedom of *not* knowing, of being unavailable. Besides, if there was an emergency, there were plenty of other lawyers in their firm who were on call.

'Tell me about yourself then,' she challenged Sam.

'What would you like to know?'

How often do you take home women you've just met?

No, even if he was inclined to tell her, which she doubted, she had no interest in those statistics. Instead, she said, 'What would you like me to know about you?'

Sam shook his head. 'You lawyers take the cake. Answering a question with another question. Playing it cautious every step of the way.'

'Well, I'm not going to ask you what school you went to, or how old you are,' she said tightly. 'But I could ask how you feel about living out here.'

'And I'd happily tell you. I love it. I wouldn't stay here if I didn't.'

'And what do you love about it?'

He shrugged. 'The people, the town. Owning my own business, setting my own goals and my own timetable.'

That made sense. Jenna could imagine the rewards of a grazier's lifestyle, the benefits of independence, while remaining connected to the community. But she couldn't help also remembering her own experience of life in the bush …

'So the drought doesn't get you down?'

'The drought's an issue, for sure, and it's certainly given me more than a few headaches. But the good seasons will come again. In the meantime I guess I see the drought as—'

'A challenge?' supplied Jenna before Sam could finish the sentence.

'Exactly. And who doesn't like a good challenge?'

As Sam said this, he slowed the vehicle and turned off

the road, crossing a metal grid and driving between two tall, white gateposts. Jenna saw a sign as they whizzed past, bearing the name *Fenton*.

'There's probably a place in England called Fenton, isn't there?' she asked.

'Yeah. My great grandfather was born there and he was a traditionalist when it came to naming his property. Apparently, Fenton's a tiny place in Cambridgeshire. Right next to the town of Pidley.'

'I guess you're lucky he wasn't born in Pidley.'

They were both grinning at this as Sam pulled up in front of a long, low homestead, gleaming white in the moonlight.

Oh, my gosh. The house was lovely, with deep verandahs and bay windows and a carefully tended garden. Somehow Jenna had been expecting a much more modest place, but Fenton homestead was grand and gracious.

Sam was out of the car quickly. She heard his footsteps on the gravel and then he was opening the door for her. She felt the night air on her face, caught the scent of roses and lavender from the garden.

'Thank you,' she said as she got out. And then, perhaps it was her lovely gown, or the moonlight, or the handsome man gallantly opening a door for her and making her feel like a princess in a fairy tale … she lifted her face to kiss his cheek. And somehow that was all that was needed before his arms slipped around her and he was drawing her in. Holding her close to his hard chest, to his even harder thighs.

His lips were warm and welcoming, and their first kiss felt as natural as a sunrise and as exciting as summer lightning. And that was before urgency took hold, deepening the kiss, heating it into a wild fire, sending sparks shooting through Jenna, hot and hard.

No words were needed now. When Sam took her hand, they almost broke into a run to reach the house.

He had to stop at the front door to unlock it and they grabbed the opportunity for another impatient kiss. Once inside, a light flicked on and Jenna was aware of a spacious, comfortable living room with high ceilings and deep windows and an unmistakable touch of elegance. But décor was not her priority right now, not when Sam was kissing her again.

'Minx,' he murmured as he gathered her in. 'I was planning to be a gentleman. A little light seduction.'

'I don't need a gentleman.' And she certainly didn't need seduction. Sam Twist had been seducing her all evening, with his mesmerising smiles, with his winning words. His mere presence had been enough to keep Jenna at a smoulder. Now that smoulder had burst into flames.

Again he took her hand, this time leading her down a hallway and into a bedroom. She gained a fast impression of French doors and gleaming timber flooring, of charcoal grey walls and a massive bed before she was distracted by Sam tugging his bow tie undone and shrugging out of his coat.

She might have found the whole undressing thing awkward without Sam's smile and his easy manner. Instead it was a simple matter of helping him with his shirt buttons to discover the sleek muscularity beneath. *Oh, man.*

Then Jenna was slipping off her shoes and unzipping her bridesmaid's gown. And when Sam helped her out of the dress to reveal her brand-new, ridiculously expensive lingerie, his deeply appreciative smile rendered her all kinds of confident and sexy.

Game on.

WHEN JENNA WOKE, the bedroom was filled with bright sunlight. Sam had disappeared and she lay in his bed, slowly coming to terms with the lateness of the hour and the wonder of the night that had just passed.

Wow.

Actually, there had to be a better word than wow! But right now it was all she could come up with. Wow times one hundred.

Jenna had never experienced such amazing sex, had never felt so uninhibited, so full-to-the-brim satisfied. So incredibly over-the-top happy!

One-night stands *that* good should be banned, surely? They left a girl desperate for more.

This morning, however, had brought Jenna's reality

check. There would not be any more sex with Sam and that prospect was way more depressing than it should have been.

At least, waking to this reality involved the heady aroma of coffee drifting down the hallway. Good coffee, too, if Jenna's nose was any judge.

Yikes. If Sam topped such a great night of stellar love making with a morning after of excellent coffee and a half-decent breakfast, how on earth had the man managed to remain single?

Jenna decided to get up. Somehow, breakfast in bed felt a shade too luxurious and intimate for the morning after a fling. The only clothing she had, though, was her brides-maid's dress, which seemed rather ridiculous attire for breakfast, so she helped herself to the white dress shirt Sam had left draped over a chair in the corner. She needed to roll the long sleeves up, but the shirt tails reached to mid-thigh, so that was fine.

With her face washed and her hair tidied—borrowing a brush she'd found in Sam's ensuite—she went, barefoot, down the passage, following her nose in search of the kitchen. This proved to be a lovely, sun-filled room with loads of windows offering views of the garden and beyond to rolling paddocks dotted with gum trees and mobs of sheep.

Sam, busy at the stove, dealing with a sizzling frying pan, hadn't heard her arrive, so she had a chance to check him out. To admire the back view of wide shoulders stretching the seams of his faded grey T-shirt, his lean hips and hot butt in equally faded, low-slung jeans.

Make the most of this sight, she thought with a sigh.

A black-and-white border collie, sitting patiently in a corner, ears alert, was watching Sam as he worked, watching Jenna as well.

'Good morning,' Jenna called.

Sam turned from the stove and his face broke into the sexiest grin. 'Good morning to you.' He stood there for a moment, egg-flip in hand, smiling at her, staring. 'There ought to be a law against women wearing nothing but a man's shirt,' he said as he set the egg flip aside and turned down the stove. Then he came across the room to her. 'No, I take that back. Such shirts should be compulsory when a woman looks as good as you.'

He kissed Jenna lightly, just the brush of his lips on hers, but it was enough to uncoil a bud of longing deep within her. 'How'd you sleep?' he asked with a cheeky, knowing smile.

She narrowed her eyes at him, but she was smiling too. 'I hardly slept at all. There were so many interruptions.'

'Didn't hear you complaining.'

'No.' More than likely she'd been moaning with pleasure. Remembering just how abandoned and uninhibited she'd been in his bed, Jenna felt her cheeks grow hot. She decided it might be smart to change the subject. 'You were up early.'

'I had stock to feed.'

Sam said this simply, but Jenna knew that a need to feed his stock meant there must be almost no pasture left for grazing. She also guessed he was probably a lot more worried about this than he'd let on.

She nodded towards the border collie who'd been watching them intently. 'Who's this?' she asked.

'This is Gerry. Short for Geraldine.' The dog's ears pricked up as soon as she heard her name mentioned. 'Here, girl.'

She padded towards Sam, tail wagging, eyes bright and he stroked her silky, black-and-white head. 'This is Jenna, Gerry. Say hello.'

Obediently, Gerry lifted a paw.

'Aww …' Jenna couldn't help but be enchanted. 'Hello, Gerry,' she said as she shook the proffered paw. 'You're beautiful.'

'My mother left her behind when she moved to Queensland,' said Sam. 'We used to have her brother, Tom, as well.'

'Tom and Gerry?' Jenna asked with a grin.

'Yeah.'

'Is she a working dog?' she asked as Sam turned back to the frying pan.

'She worked when she was younger. She was brilliant with the sheep, actually, and she would still be useful, if I needed her, but she's more or less retired now. By rights, she shouldn't be in the house, but I have soft spot for the old girl.'

'I'm sure she's good company.'

Flipping bacon in the pan, Sam nodded.

'That smells so good,' Jenna said next. 'So does the coffee.'

'The coffee's ready. Coming right up.' Transforming back into perfect-host mode, Sam drew a chair for Jenna at a table set for two.

'Can I do anything to help?' She wasn't used to having a man wait on her. 'Make toast or something?'

'Okay, thanks.' He handed her a red-and-white-striped mug. 'Here's your coffee to keep you going.' Retrieving a bread knife from a drawer, he held that out, too. 'If you don't mind doing the slicing, there's a loaf of sourdough from our local bakery.'

'Yum.'

It was way too convivial really, Jenna decided, with Sam at the stove while she sliced the lovely fresh bread and dropped it into the toaster. It was almost as if they'd known each other for ages. Which wasn't at all how a one-night stand should feel.

That was the trouble with a weekend in the country. She couldn't just say thanks and see you later and then catch an Uber home.

STRAIGHT AFTER BREAKFAST—A totally delicious breakfast of

bacon and scrambled eggs with fried tomatoes, not to mention perfect coffee and scrumptious toast topped with delicious, locally made marmalade—it seemed important to Jenna to make her position clear, pointing out that she needed to be on her way.

Fortunately, Sam made no attempt to persuade her otherwise, although his smile may have lost a little of its spark. Obviously, he was sensible enough to know there was no point in delaying her return into town. And that was good. Great.

Enough with the fun and frivolity.

By leaving now, Jenna could be safely back in her own inner-Melbourne apartment by mid-afternoon, which would give her enough time to catch up on a good chunk of the work she'd missed. All in all, a prompt departure was a perfect ending to a fabulous weekend.

Of course, Jenna felt a tad weird getting back into her bridesmaid's dress for the return into Wirralong, but she had no option. She consoled herself that at least, if townsfolk saw her and guessed what she'd been up to, she wouldn't be around to hear their gossip.

As Sam started up the SUV, she chose not to look back at his lovely homestead. And it seemed that neither she nor Sam had much to say as they set off. She supposed there was little point in idle chatter when they had no plans to ever see each other again. That was the nature of a one-night stand. It was what she'd wanted.

Wasn't it?

Mostly Jenna stared ahead at the track, but she couldn't help catching details of the property that she'd missed last night in the dark. Now she noted sheds, one of which was probably for shearing, and there were silos, too, for storing grain. But it was the dry, sparsely grassed paddocks that held her attention.

She was working out a suitably sympathetic comment about the drought when Sam slowed the vehicle and then came to a complete stop. Leaning an elbow on the window sill, he stared out at a sunburnt paddock sprinkled with sheep and with crows circling above.

He dropped a swear word, only just loud enough for Jenna to catch.

'What's the matter?' she asked.

'Looks like a ewe's down.' Already Sam had opened his door and was climbing out. 'Sorry, Jenna, but I need to check on her. All these ewes are pregnant. She could be in trouble.'

'Yes, of course.'

Without another glance her way, Sam set off, yanking up strands of barbed wire to duck through the fence and then striding across the paddock. He was only about a hundred metres or so away when he stopped and crouched beside what looked like a woolly bundle on the ground.

Jenna supposed he was examining the poor ewe and she wished she didn't feel quite so useless, but of course, she knew zilch about delivering baby lambs. And anyway, she didn't like her chances of successfully negotiating the barbwire fence in her high heels and long, floaty bridesmaid's dress.

Just her luck, she'd get caught up and Sam would have to rescue her as well as the poor sheep.

As she watched, Sam rose with a white and woolly bundle in his arms. A lamb, surely? No, possibly two lambs.

Yes. Now he was coming back across the paddock, and he seemed to have a lamb hooked under both arms. Jumping out of the car, Jenna crossed to the fence where she put her foot on a lower strand of wire and lifted the top one so that Sam, with his arms full, could get through.

'Thanks.' He spoke cheerfully enough, but his smile was grim.

Jenna looked at the helpless little woolly creatures he carried. The lambs' eyes were closed, their little bodies limp, legs dangling. 'Is their mother dead?' she asked.

Sam nodded. ''Fraid so. And these guys are pretty damn weak.'

'Poor little things. Can you bottle feed them?'

'Yeah, I'll have to.' He shot her a cautious glance. 'But, I'll need to feed them soon. Now, in fact. I'm not sure they'll last much longer.'

'Yes, of course. Let me open a car door for you. Will you put them on the backseat?'

He nodded. 'Thanks.'

Jenna couldn't help being touched by the gentle way Sam handled the fragile lambs. As they drove back to the homestead, she kept twisting in her seat to keep an eye on them as they lay huddled together. One lamb opened its golden-brown eyes and seemed to look at her.

'You're going to be okay, little guys,' she couldn't help telling them. 'Sam will look after you.'

'Sam will do his best,' Sam added tersely.

He was tense, Jenna could tell. She wondered how many times this had happened already this season.

Once again, dark memories threatened and she shuddered.

Don't, she scolded herself. She needed to keep talking, to stay in the present, not the past. 'Lambs are usually born in winter, aren't they?'

Sam nodded. 'Usually, but I didn't want to risk leaving it that late this year. Winters are hard enough for newborn lambs, even in a good year. But we always lose some, and when there's drought as well and the ewes are weak—' He gave a shrug. 'The forecasters were talking up the potential for early rain. I took a gamble and crossed the ewes earlier than usual.'

'Farming's always a bit of a gamble, isn't it?'

His face tightened. 'I guess. We can do our best to make our properties sustainable, but we need Mother Nature to come to the party.'

Yes, she thought, and despite her best efforts to resist, she couldn't help remembering her childhood. Her parents' tight, grim faces and the hushed and anxious conversations in the homestead kitchen at night, when they'd thought that Jenna and her sister, Sally, were asleep. The Christmas presents that Jenna and Sally had known were recycled from the second-hand charity shop, and still smelled old, despite their mum's efforts to 'freshen them up.'

Sam pulled up again in front of the homestead and Jenna mentally slammed a door on those memories.

'Would you like me to take one?' she asked, as he opened the back door again to retrieve the first lamb.

Sam's amused gaze slid over her. 'You wouldn't want to spoil that lovely dress.'

'I don't mind. The dress will clean.'

'You sure?'

'Absolutely.'

He shrugged. 'Okay, then. Thanks.'

It was only as Jenna carefully lifted the lamb out that she realised how very weak it was. The poor thing hardly had the strength to lift its head, and she could feel its rib cage and the hammer of its heartbeat beneath her hand. As she followed Sam back into the house, to the kitchen, she hated to think that those frantic little beats might grow weaker until they stopped.

SAM SPREAD A newspaper in a corner of the kitchen and set his lamb down while he fetched the colostrum replacement that the newborns needed within their first twenty-four hours. Then he found the bottles and teats.

Returning, he discovered Jenna sitting cross-legged on the floor. And what an amazing picture she made, in that damned bridesmaid's dress, with Gerry next to her, and a lamb cradled in one arm, while she gently patted the other lamb on the floor beside her.

Bloody hell. The sight was enough to stop a man in his tracks, not merely because the picture was so damn beautiful, but because it didn't make any kind of sense. Wasn't this the city girl, the high-flying corporate lawyer? The girl who was dead afraid to hang around in Wirralong for a minute longer than was strictly necessary, who had to get out before a speck of outback dust could settle on her sexy high heels?

Sam had expected to find Jenna impatiently pacing the kitchen, anxious to be on her way again.

Instead this girl looked up at him with big worried eyes, as if the survival of these lambs was as important to her as it was to him. 'I don't suppose you need help with mixing the formula?' she asked.

'No, thanks,' Sam said, bemused. 'I have sachets of colostrum supplement, all measured and ready to go.' He found the stainless steel mixing bowl and beaters and set to work, adding warm water to the powder and then mixing.

The whole time, however, his head was filled with

thoughts of Jenna. Jenna last night, winning him with her smile, enchanting him as she danced in his arms. Jenna in his bed, naked and wild. Intoxicating.

In actual fact, he'd been trying, unsuccessfully, to *not* think about Jenna ever since he'd woken this morning. For ages after he'd roused from sleep to find her lying beside him, deceptively innocent, he'd lain there, too, like some kind of lovesick fool. Staring at her sleep-mussed golden hair and soft pink lips. At the fine blue veins on her eyelids, at the soft sweep of lashes on her cheeks. The bare, kissable shoulder peeking above the sheet.

So gobsmackingly lovely. So bloody tempting ... especially when he knew every soft, sweet dip and curve that lay beneath that sheet. It had taken every ounce of his self-control to leave without waking her. It was almost as if she'd cast a spell on him.

But how crazy was that? He'd had great sex before. Plenty of times, thank you.

Of course, he'd never had sex with a bridesmaid straight after a wedding. Perhaps the elusive, extra 'something' that was bothering him this morning was merely a stray romantic vibe, a hangover from a ceremony where he'd watched his best friend tie the knot and drive off into happy-ever-after.

Whatever. Sam had no plans for ever after. He'd grown up as an only child, and managing on his own had become a habit. These days, he'd never felt the need for constant company. Instead, he'd discovered the benefits of playing the field, never concentrating on one particular woman. Variety was the spice of life, wasn't it?

For sure, just as soon as Jenna was out of the district, he'd be back to his easy come, easy go self.

Okay, with that mental tussle sorted and the bottles filled and warmed, Sam fitted the teats and returned to the lambs. Jenna was cradling the smaller one in her arms, almost as if it was a human baby.

These lambs should, by rights, be standing. There was a danger of them developing aspiration pneumonia if they drank the milk lying down, but these newborns were as weak as any Sam had seen and their legs were too powerless to support them.

He handed a bottle to Jenna. 'You happy to do the honours?'

'Yes, please.' She offered her lamb the teat. 'Come on, little Molly,' she urged it gently.

'Molly?' Sam asked, as he settled with its twin.

'Well, I took a look and I think she's a girl. Oh, good, she's sucking already. What a relief. Good girl, Molly.'

Once again, Sam found himself staring. Jenna seemed totally absorbed, as if she genuinely cared about the tiny scrap of animal in her arms.

'Have you done this before?' he couldn't help asking.

She looked a little startled and a tide of pink rose from her neck to her cheeks. 'I—I might have, years and years ago, when I was very young.'

'Well, it's not a crime, Jenna. You don't have to look guilty. I just didn't expect you'd—' Sam stopped, without finishing the sentence. Jenna clearly had hang-ups about country life, but he didn't want to add to her obvious discomfort.

'Don't worry,' she said softly. 'I didn't expect I'd want to do this either.' She gave him a shy, almost girlish smile. 'I've surprised myself.'

'Maybe you'll have to hang around to make sure this pair get through their first twenty-four hours.' *Shit.* He hadn't meant to say that. Sam braced himself for her inevitable angry retort.

To his surprise, Jenna smiled. 'Maybe I will.'

Stunned, he could only stare harder. And now Jenna looked puzzled, too, as if she also couldn't quite believe what she'd just said.

'It's the lambs,' she said. 'You're right. I'd really like to see them grow stronger before I leave.'

'Well, yeah, sure,' Sam mumbled as he recovered. 'You're very welcome. So, you mean you'd stay another night?'

'Well, I'd—ah—still need to check out from the hotel and collect my things, but do you think a one-night stand can—ah—'

'Stretch to two nights?'

'Yeah. I don't want to impose.'

'Believe me, Jenna. Another night with you is no imposition.'

She kept her gaze lowered. 'A two-night stand?'

Sounds perfect. Sam didn't voice this thought, but when Jenna looked up, he offered her his warmest smile.

Chapter Five

I T WAS THE lambs' fault, of course it was.

But even with this *almost* valid excuse, Jenna couldn't quite believe she'd just committed herself to another night in the outback. How could she be so impulsive? So irresponsible? What about all the work piling up?

Crazy thing was, even though she blamed the lambs, she wasn't even particularly maternal. In fact, she was pretty certain she'd skipped the mothering gene, but these helpless baby lambs had stolen her heart. They were so sweet and vulnerable, so woolly and white and perfect.

Her interest in Sam could not be a factor. Well, not a very strong factor, she tried to tell herself, valiantly ignoring the glaring reality that another night with Sam almost certainly meant a repeat of last night's glorious sexathon.

So, once the lambs were fed and put to sleep in a box lined with straw that Sam set in a shady spot on the verandah, he dropped Jenna back into town to collect her car and her spare clothes. By now, her bridesmaid's dress was covered in dirty streaks and milky dribbles, so it was no surprise that the girl on the hotel's reception desk had eyes out on stalks when Jenna strolled in, trying to look nonchalant.

'Sorry I'm late to check out,' Jenna told her. 'There was an emergency—out on a farm—newborn lambs.' She flapped her hands in an attempt to fill the obvious gaps in this dodgy story.

For sure the girl would know that Jenna had no expertise in caring for newborn lambs and that she was, in fact, a lawyer from Melbourne. Wirralong was a very small country town, after all, and no-one could stay incognito for longer than five minutes.

Nevertheless, Jenna flashed the girl her brightest smile. 'I'll just clean up now and be back down in ten.'

Luckily, Jenna was used to a quick turnaround for showering and changing her clothes. As good as her word, she was downstairs again inside the promised ten minutes, changed into a T-shirt and jeans and with her overnight bag packed. 'I'll pay extra for the late check out,' she offered.

'No worries, it's okay.' The girl gave her a knowing smile that might have included a wink. 'We don't have a booking for your room for this evening.'

Jenna beamed at her. 'That's great. Thanks.' She left a hefty tip anyway.

IT WAS ONLY as she drove in her own little, peacock-blue, city sedan back out along the road to Fenton that Jenna began to have second thoughts about this latest decision, and then third and fourth thoughts. Bloody hell, a two-night stand was a crazy idea. Total madness, no question.

If she came to her senses and headed back to Melbourne now, she could still be home before dark and she would have a full evening to catch up on her work. She should ring Sam and explain. He was bound to agree it was sensible.

Except that she didn't have Sam's number—an oversight that would never have occurred if she'd been using her phone. Damn it, she really should put an end to that stupid ban right now.

Without another moment's hesitation, Jenna pulled off the road and reached for her phone. Her lifeline. Normally, it would have been plugged in and ready for action. It was sheer nonsense to have left it turned off.

Except …

Oh, help. The weirdest shadow of doubt hovered as her thumb hesitated over the 'on' button.

And then fresh thoughts tumbled in. Maybe … damn it, maybe just one weekend off wouldn't ruin her career. And maybe, if she was completely honest, she just couldn't resist stealing one more night with Sam Twist.

JENNA FELT STRANGELY light-hearted as she dropped her phone onto the passenger's seat and continued down the road.

Driving back to Sam's property in her own car, in normal clothes and in daylight was quite a different experience from the previous night's journey. Without the distraction of Sam by her side, she was more conscious of her surroundings.

There were so many things she'd forgotten about the countryside, like the sheer beauty of a wide-open, clear blue sky and the allure of distant purple hills. The quintessential Aussie charm of kookaburras perched on a road sign, of kangaroos resting in a gum tree's shade.

Lowering a window, she drew a deep breath. The air was warm and dusty, but tinged with a minty and fresh hint of eucalyptus. Not a whiff of petrol fumes.

Whoa. Hold it right there.

The mere fact that she was going back to Fenton was no reason to get carried away. It was time to give herself a stern lecture. Time to remember that idyllic scenery and nostalgic scents were all very well. But she also knew from painful experience that the reality of actually *living* in the country was a completely different, much sadder story.

SAM WAS SURPRISED when he heard Jenna's car heading back down the track to the homestead. After he'd dropped her in Wirralong at the hotel, he'd half expected—no, he'd almost *fully* expected—her to call and tell him she'd changed her mind and would be returning to Melbourne. He'd even been prepared for the possibility that she might simply disappear without any contact, hightailing it back to the city, never to be seen or heard of again.

Instead, almost miraculously, here Jenna was, back. For another night. And Sam couldn't help staring as she climbed out of her tiny car, all long legs in skinny jeans and a scoop-necked, black T-shirt that clung to her in all the right places. She'd done something with her hair, too, arranging it in a loose, golden knot that let curling tendrils escape.

Sam's breathing hitched. Other parts of him reacted as well. All day he'd thought of little else but Jenna.

In his bed last night she'd dropped the corporate lawyer facade to show him the real woman beneath. Gorgeous, earthy, sexy as hell. And now, those memories were driving him crazy.

But she'd come back and no doubt he was grinning like a maniac.

What the hell had happened to Cool Dude Twist?

It took a deliberate effort to lower the wattage on his smile as he sent her a wave and strolled towards her. 'Good timing,' he called in his most casual drawl. 'The lambs are ready for another feed.'

SITTING ON THE verandah steps with Sam, holding their woolly charges in their laps as they fed them, Jenna was sure an avowed city woman should not have enjoyed the experience. But the strange truth was, she felt happier than she had in a long time.

Surprisingly relaxed, she allowed herself to relive one of the few truly happy memories from her childhood when she'd been about seven and had cared for another pet lamb, another Molly, that she'd loved with all her heart.

Jenna had watched the Molly of her childhood grow stronger and stronger, becoming frolicsome and playful and so-o-o cute. She could remember the pride she'd felt in knowing that she'd saved the lamb's life, the wonderful sense of responsibility, of connection to another living creature.

Molly would be there to greet her when she came off the school bus and, as far as Jenna was concerned, that lamb had been even more fun than a puppy. She'd been heartbroken when her parents had insisted that Molly was old enough to return to the flock.

Now, to her surprise, once the lambs were fed, Sam served afternoon tea. Jenna almost laughed in his face. She'd half expected, half hoped he would race her off to bed for a matinee. Instead, he was serving proper, old-fashioned leaf tea in a teapot and actual scones—albeit from the freezer, which he'd reheated in the microwave.

'These are delicious,' Jenna told him. 'But I can't quite believe it. I'm sorry, Sam, but I've never met a guy who keeps homemade scones in his freezer.'

'Yeah, but this guy's mother came back last Christmas and threw herself into a frenzy of baking, leaving him with a freezer chockers to the brim.'

'Right.' Jenna supposed this was an example of the old saying that you could take the woman out of the country, but you couldn't take the country out of the woman.

'Your mum must have loved her life here.' As Jenna said this she was also thinking of her own mum, who'd only flourished after she'd left the outback and moved to Brisbane.

Looking up, she caught Sam watching her with a thoughtful, curious expression.

'My mother did love it here,' he said. 'But her life wasn't all tea and scones. She helped Dad on the property, taking care of most of the paperwork, but she was also an artist. One of those sheds out there was her studio, and most of the paintings in this house are hers.'

'Wow.' Jenna had admired the paintings, mostly landscapes in bold colours and strong lines with a very contemporary vibe. 'They're wonderful. I looked at the signatures, but I didn't recognise the name.'

'Verity Holden,' he said. 'Mum's maiden name.'

Ah, that made sense. 'Your mother's very talented,' Jenna said.

'She is, yes. And her friends in the district were an interesting lot, too. Her best friend was the local doctor.'

'Right.' Jenna supposed this was Sam's way of pointing his finger at her narrow-minded view of country women, but she could do without the lecture, thank you. She knew from personal experience there were many sides to rural life, including those not so rosy.

'Mum left after Dad died,' Sam added. 'It wasn't the same for her then.'

'No, I suppose it wouldn't be.' Jenna knew she should probably make some sort of polite enquiry about Sam's father, but the last thing she wanted now was a discussion of fathers and death. Instead, she said, 'Do you have brothers or sisters?'

Sam shook his head. 'I'm the one and only.'

'What is it that parents with only kids say? They got it right the first time?'

'Something like that. I think perfection might have been mentioned.'

She smiled, looked around at the lovely homestead, the view of paddocks through the windows. 'Don't tell me you do everything, though—all the housework *and* the farm work.'

Sam shrugged. 'I have a woman, Hettie Green, who comes once a week to vacuum and dust and the odd bit of ironing. She's brilliant. And I hire people when I need extra help—shearers, fencers and the like.'

But it must be lonely, still, living here all on your own. Jenna didn't voice this thought. Sam certainly showed no signs of loneliness. She opted to change the subject. 'And what does a sheep farmer do on a Sunday afternoon?'

'On *this* Sunday afternoon, this sheep farmer distributes more stock feed.'

'I see.'

'You want to come?'

Perhaps if Sam's invitation had not been accompanied by another of his sexy smiles, Jenna might have found it easier to resist. But the weird thing was that she did feel inclined to go with him. Mostly, she just wanted to hang around, enjoying his company and watching the easy way he moved.

Her usual work days were filled with self-important males strutting about in stuffy business suits, but Sam in an old T-shirt and battered jeans was an infinitely superior sight, especially as she had firsthand, intimate knowledge of the rippling muscles beneath his clothes. And, yeah, she was dead-curious to watch him handle his stock, or swing a bale of hay onto a bulky shoulder.

But she said, 'I should probably check my emails.' Because, truly, it was time to be sensible.

Sam pulled a face. 'I'm pretty sure it's illegal to check emails on a Sunday afternoon.'

'Illegal?' Jenna tried to scoff, to glare at him, but she couldn't help smiling back. 'Are you quite sure?'

He gave a slow nod. 'Can't have a lawyer breaking the law.' And then he came towards Jenna, and without further warning, he reached for her and drew her against him and he was solid and warm and very, very male. His mouth was on hers, gentle and hard at once, coaxing and demanding, tender and hot.

'Oh, very well,' she murmured as she wound her arms around him and nestled closer. 'Because you asked so nicely—no emails.'

IT REALLY WAS the pleasantest of afternoons. As the sun rolled westwards, tinting the land with russet and gold, they drove around various paddocks in a ute with bales of stock feed loaded in its tray-back. Which gave Jenna ample opportunity to watch Sam in action, hefting bales out of the ute and over fences, spreading the hay out evenly.

There was nothing haphazard about this process, she soon discovered. As they drove between stops, Sam outlined a few of his drought management strategies, explaining that while there were paddocks that looked as if they still carried feed, it was important not to over-graze these, as this would lead to loss of soil, nutrients and seed.

He also explained that he'd diversified in recent years and kept a small herd of beef cattle, as well as the sheep. 'They're further out,' he said. 'Closer to the river.'

He went on to explain the ongoing need to regularly weigh his stock, assessing and recording their condition and making sure they weren't over or under fed.

'So there's plenty of planning involved,' Jenna suggested.

'Hell, yeah. The best way to survive a drought—the only way, actually—is to have your plans in place long before there's any sign of the country drying out.'

'It's all quite scientific.'

He slid her a cheeky smile. 'Yeah, but it's okay, Jenna. I'm not trying to impress you.'

'Oh?' She couldn't help responding with a playful smile of her own. 'So how would you behave if you *were* trying to impress me?'

This time Sam chuckled and his grey eyes flashed. 'I'll save that for later.'

Zap.

Heat rushed straight to Jenna's core as she thought about later—tonight, in Sam's bed—and she was so hot and horny she could scarcely sit still.

With dusk, the pleasant afternoon drifted into a blissful evening. They fed the lambs again—and the ram, the stronger of the two, was actually able to stand now. Jubilant, Jenna gave Sam a high five and then she suggested that she should cook dinner to thank him for his hospitality.

In the end, they worked together, concocting a simple pasta with a sauce from ingredients Jenna found in Sam's fridge—tomatoes, olives, capers, a little basil from a pot at the back door, plus a generous sprinkling of parmesan. Music in the background played popular songs from the past decade and the kitchen was redolent with the aromas of tomato and basil.

Jenna wouldn't allow herself to dwell on how enjoyable this was, with the two of then behaving almost like a staid, established couple.

At least there was nothing staid about the hunger she felt for Sam. Or the way, as they chopped and stirred, that he would stop her, every once in a while, reeling her in for a kiss or a sexy nibble, keeping her at a high, bone-melting simmer.

SAM WAXED LYRICAL when he tasted their meal. 'I hardly ever eat vegetarian, but I reckon I could go for this any day of the week.'

'It certainly helps when you wash it down with such a lovely red wine,' Jenna agreed as she savoured another deep sip of the first class, locally produced shiraz Sam had selected from his cellar.

After the meal, they took their glasses with the last of the wine into the lounge room and settled on the sofa. With just a couple of lamps turned low and the night closing in outside, it was all very cosy and might even have been relaxing without the distracting flame of longing that kept Jenna on edge.

She was surprised she didn't also feel twitchy and itching to open her laptop, but she wouldn't allow herself to think about the mountain of work waiting for her in the morning. Instead, she made a point of tucking up her feet and curling comfortably in a corner of the sofa, while she and Sam chatted quietly.

He told her about a trip he'd made to South America, where he'd visited grazing properties on the Pampas and had tasted the most amazing food roasted on an Argentinian barbecue, called an asado, and how he'd then continued by ship from Ushuaia to Antarctica.

'How awesome is that?' Jenna was genuinely impressed. 'I've only been overseas with my work, and I kept to the big cities—New York, London, Stockholm.'

'Not Paris?' He looked amused as he asked this.

'Not yet. But I don't think I'd want to go to Paris for work. I'm sure I'd just want to shop and look at art galleries and have fun.'

Sam grinned. 'That's a relief.'

'Why?'

'You're not quite the workaholic I feared.'

Oh, but I am, Jenna almost assured him, but she didn't want to spoil the relaxed mood. And, for a giddy moment, she even allowed herself to imagine being in Paris with Sam. Walking arm in arm with him beside the Seine at dusk, dining on *foie gras* in a centuries-old café that was dripping with atmosphere, staying in a chic little hotel in Saint

Germain, the arrondissement so beloved by writers and artists.

Bloody hell, Jenna. Get a grip.

'I'm sure the lambs will need feeding during the night,' she said, dragging herself back to their current reality.

''Fraid so. But you don't need to get up.'

'Of course I do. I can't claim that I'm staying here on the pretext that the lambs' survival is all important and then blithely sleep through their feeds.'

'In that case …' Sam sent her another of his dangerous smiles, as he rose from the sofa and held out his hand to her. 'We'd better make sure you get to bed early.'

Chapter Six

A T LAST.

Sam wasn't sure how he'd got through the day without dragging Jenna off to bed. There'd been several occasions when he'd almost tested his luck and he'd been pretty confident she wouldn't have knocked him back, but this was a strictly casual affair, so there was little point in acting like a lovestruck fool.

After all, he and Jenna had both been very clear that this was temporary. And with a city sophisticate like Jenna Matthews there was always a danger of overplaying his hand.

So, Sam had played it cool, or as cool as he could manage, given that Jenna's company all day had been a constant and maddening distraction. And now, as they came to bed, she was wearing a skimpy, blue silk nightie with spaghetti straps that showed off her perfect cleavage and beautiful pale shoulders.

All he wanted now was to rip that teasing scrap of blue silk straight off her, to have her up close and naked at last and to once again explore every intoxicating inch of her soft skin and sweet curves.

Luckily, no ripping was needed.

'I have no idea why I even bothered to put this on,' Jenna said as she slipped between the sheets, and with a saucy grin, she sat up again and hauled the nightie over her head before tossing it in a high arc to land in a dark corner.

And then she turned to Sam, offering him a flash of soft, smooth, deliciously pale skin, of lush, pink-tipped breasts. A moment he would doubtless remember forever.

AT SOME UNGODLY hour they got up to feed the lambs. Sam had moved their straw-lined box into the laundry for the night, but it was still cold in the early hours and he offered Jenna a football jersey to wear, for which she was grateful.

'You need a nightcap? A hot drink?' he asked, once the lambs were settled again.

She shook her head. 'No, I'm fine, thanks.' But she felt sad, thinking of the many nights ahead when Sam would have to get up and perform this task without her.

Perhaps he sensed that she felt a bit down as they climbed into bed again, Jenna having shed the jersey. He turned towards her with one of his trademark smiles and actually began to recite:

'There once was a girl at a wedding
Whom the best man fancied bedding.
But she discovered a lamb
That had lost its mam—'

He paused for a moment, obviously hunting for a last line, when Jenna jumped in.

'And now, back to the city she's heading.'

'Minx.' His smile dimmed somewhat. 'You've gone and ruined a beautiful story.'

'No, no,' Jenna protested. 'The story would only be ruined if the best man hadn't bedded the girl, but I can assure you he did. And he was beyond awesome.'

'And she was smoking-hot.'

At least they were both chuckling as they rolled towards each other again, but the laughter soon died as their lips met and their mouths meshed and their kiss quickly deepened.

Once again, making love with Sam felt very, very right. But now Jenna also sensed that the tempo had changed. There wasn't quite the same urgency. The mood was sensual rather than electric, leisurely and tender and generous.

She couldn't remember ever feeling quite so moved. If Sam had thrilled her previously, now he touched her soul. And afterwards, they nestled close as if they needed to stay in contact while they drifted back to sleep.

Such intimacy was beyond Jenna's experience, an indulgence she'd never previously permitted herself. She was quite sure it was dangerous, but she couldn't help relishing the loveliness of it, savouring every precious moment, while madly hoping that she wasn't falling in love.

At least she knew that her life would be safely back to normal in the morning.

SAM ROSE AT the crack of dawn, but this time Jenna made sure she was up just as early. While he made a quick tour of inspection of the paddocks closest to the homestead, she showered and stowed her things in her car, ready for a speedy takeoff. She aimed to leave just as soon as she'd given the lambs a final feed.

Neither she nor Sam had much to say. They were both rather subdued, actually, although there was cause for celebration when Molly rose, somewhat shakily, to stand on all fours beside her brother.

Jenna was ecstatic. 'Oh, you clever, clever girl!'

She told herself it had been worth the risky decision to spend a second night at Fenton just to witness this fabulous achievement. The state of her emotions and her feelings for the lambs' owner were another matter entirely. Hopefully, getting back to work would soon cure her.

'The lambs should be fine now, shouldn't they?' Jenna asked, as she breakfasted on coffee and toast, having warned Sam that she must be on her way and didn't need another big meal.

Sam nodded. 'I reckon they'll both be—' He stopped and frowned, turning his head as if listening. 'Sounds like a car coming.'

'Oh?' At first Jenna couldn't hear anything, but then she caught the hum of a motor in the distance. Before long, it was definitely clear that a vehicle was coming towards them. 'A good time for me to head off then,' she said.

'No need to rush. Finish your breakfast.'

But Jenna was quite sure that she should be on her way. The Monday morning traffic in Melbourne would be hellacious and she was also certain that Sam didn't need one of his curious neighbours finding her here at this early hour, enjoying a cosy breakfast with him.

'It's okay,' she said, rising. 'I'll take the toast with me and eat it in the car. It's high time I got out of your hair.'

Sam looked uncertain, but after a slight hesitation during which he seemed to be tossing up possibilities, he gave in with a shrug and a nod. 'Right then.'

There was no point in lingering over goodbyes. Jenna held out her hand. 'Thanks, Sam.'

His mouth tilted in a half smile that didn't quite reach his eyes. 'Come here,' he said, ignoring the hand she offered and pulling her into a hug. A wholehearted, glorious bear hug, like nothing she'd ever experienced.

Oh, God, don't let me cry. Jenna knew she would never forget the warmth of Sam's strong arms around her and the fierce way he held her to him, as if she was the most precious thing in the world. She was blinking madly as he released her, as she picked up the marmalade toast and her car keys.

'Bye,' she said, relieved that he wouldn't expect a farewell speech.

Sam was ever the gentleman, though, and he walked with

her to the front door. They were crossing through the lounge room, when tyres crunched on the gravel drive outside.

Through glass panels in the front door, Jenna saw a black sedan pull up and a man get out. Middle aged, he was short of stature and overweight, and wearing a shiny blue suit and tie.

Even at this distance, Jenna could sense his officious manner. He looked more like a banker or a city real estate agent than a visiting grazier. An uneasy chill snaked down her spine.

'I have no idea who this could be,' Sam said, frowning.

Jenna hid the toast she'd been carrying behind her back as the new arrival mounted the steps and crossed the verandah. Sam went to answer the door.

'Mr Samuel Twist?' The visitor on the doorstep spoke loudly and managed to make the simple question sound menacing.

'Yes?' Sam responded tersely.

The fellow looked Sam up and down and then, with an uncomfortable smile, held out an extra-large yellow envelope.

'What's this?' asked Sam without accepting the envelope.

'Mr Twist, I'm here to present a formal writ served against you by the courts—'

'What the hell?'

The pompous fellow ignored Sam's interruption. 'A writ for the destruction of property and trespass.'

Oh, God. Jenna saw Sam stiffen, saw his fists clench and, for a shaky moment, she thought he was going to land a punch on the fellow's smug pink face. Instead, Sam inhaled sharply, straightened his shoulders, and drew himself taller than ever.

'Thank you,' he said tightly, but with unmistakable dignity. And then, with obvious reluctance, he accepted the envelope and promptly closed the door in the caller's face.

Sam didn't turn back to Jenna, but stood very still. Through the door's glass panels, she could see the little man dithering on the door mat for a moment or two, looking up and down the length of the verandah, before turning and heading back down the steps to his car.

It was only as the car door slammed and the motor started up that Sam turned, and by then he looked fit to kill someone.

'The bastards. They really think they can get away with this.' He tossed the envelope into a nearby armchair, then stood, with his hands braced on his hips and his jaw hard and belligerent, as he scowled at a spot on the carpet.

'Sounds like you might need a good lawyer.' Jenna spoke gently, keeping her tone light.

He gave a vehement shake of his head. 'I don't need a lawyer. This is a load of bullshit. I don't need anyone.'

She was still holding the toast behind her back and it was hardly the right moment to eat it, so she set it carefully on the coffee table, licked a blob of marmalade from her thumb.

'Sam, I—'

'It's okay,' he cut in, adding a sharp, forbidding glare. 'Thanks all the same, Jenna, but I don't need a lawyer. I know my rights. This is my family's property and, I tell you, this is bloody nonsense.'

Jenna knew very well that having a writ issued in this manner was not nonsense, and the consequences of stubbornly ignoring such an official summons were, potentially, severe.

'Sam,' she said gently. 'I think you should—'

'And I certainly don't need a lecture,' he snapped. 'More to the point, *you* need to be on your way.'

Jenna might have been intimidated by this sudden change in Sam, but she'd dealt with plenty of scared and stubborn alpha males who'd run head first into legal brick walls. And, having spent a weekend with this man, having witnessed his dedication to this property, she also knew how deeply disturbed he must be now. Even though he was trying to brazen it out.

Trying a different tactic, she said, 'So you do know what this is about?'

Sam took his time answering. Eventually, he gave a reluctant nod. 'I have a fair idea.' He let out an exasperated sigh. 'A big mining company has taken out an Authority to Prospect that covers the whole of the river bed and it's put up a so-called security fence, which means I can't get my cattle to water.'

Now Sam threw his arms wide, palms up, in a gesture of helpless frustration. 'They had no bloody right to put that fence up. It's crazy. All the properties along the river have had access—for generations. And the water level's already as low as it's ever been. I had to walk the cattle halfway across the dry bed just to get a drink. And then these bastards went and fenced off that last access to water.'

'But the company's now saying you've damaged their property and trespassed. So what exactly did you do, Sam?'

Again he glared at her. 'I cut the bloody fence, of course.'

So. The man *was* a pirate after all.

Chapter Seven

'YOU NEED LEGAL advice, Sam.'

He was standing at the window now, still with his hands on his hips, glaring out at the vista of paddocks. 'Thanks all the same, but I'm not looking for advice.'

'I can imagine you wouldn't want advice from me,' Jenna said, in case that was what was bothering him. 'But I'm not offering.'

He turned now, his gaze fierce yet curious. 'I thought you were a hotshot lawyer?'

'That's not the point. We—you and I—have history. I know we've only spent a weekend together, but we've slept together.' Jenna saw the flash of heat in Sam's eyes as she said this and, in response, teasing flames licked at her skin.

She drew a quick breath to steady herself, to keep her thoughts from straying to the bedroom. 'It would probably be better all round if one of my colleagues helped you,' she said.

Sam's eyebrows rose ever so slightly.

Jenna persisted. Apart from any awkwardness between them, she suspected he was the kind of male who'd more easily accept advice from another man, rather than a woman. 'But, in any case, you can't just ignore this writ, Sam. It's not worth it.'

With a shrug, he turned back to the window and Jenna almost lost her patience. Foolishly perhaps, she cared about this turn of events. Cared about Sam. 'If you have a good case, the court will listen,' she said. 'But you should also have legal assistance.'

His response was another shrug. 'What's the worst that can happen?'

'If you ignore this?'

'Yes. I can't go to jail, can I?'

'No, probably not jail, not in response to a writ, at any rate. But with a big company as the plaintiff, there'd be fines and costs. I'm sure you wouldn't want the courts dipping into your bank accounts.'

He whirled around now. 'They can't touch this property?'

'I couldn't be sure about any of those details when I don't know the full story.'

Sam's broad chest rose and fell as he drew a deep breath and slowly exhaled. 'So ...' He grimaced, clearly unhappy, but perhaps realising that stubbornness had its limits. 'So where would I start, if I decided to get this legal advice?'

'Perhaps it's time you and I exchanged phone numbers after all.'

JENNA STOPPED AT a service station on the outskirts of Wirralong, where she overheard gossip that stopped her in her tracks. She was filling up her car for the return trip to Melbourne and two middle-aged rural fellows in faded jeans and battered akubras were chatting at the next bowser.

'You heard about Sam Twist?'

Alarm zapped straight through Jenna and, of course, she was immediately all ears.

'No, nothing new,' the other fellow said. 'What's happened to Sam?'

'Got himself in trouble with the law.'

'Go on.'

'It's true. Sam rang his neighbour, Monty Pickering, and Monty rang me. Caught me just before I left home. Apparently Sam's gone and cut that bloody fence that's been put up along the river.'

'Can't blame him. Bloody crazy, that fence.'

'Yeah, but he's been served a writ.'

'Blow me down.' The guy receiving this news tilted his hat back, so he could scratch at his balding forehead. 'You can't blame Sam for taking things into his own hands. They had no right to put that bloody fence up.' He gave another scratch before settling his hat in place. 'Wonder if old man Jeffries knows about this? Saw 'im last week and he was spitting chips over the way they fenced off his stretch of river.'

Jenna gave an involuntary gasp at this new piece of information. Jeffries was Cate's maiden name. The old man they referred to was almost certainly Cate's dad.

Instantly, she recalled Mr Jeffries' proud smile as he'd escorted Cate across the paddock to her waiting bridegroom. Remembered, too, the glitter of tears in his eyes when he'd paid tribute to his deceased wife during his speech at the reception.

'If Ted Jeffries hasn't heard about Sam's problems, he soon will,' the fellow full of news went on. 'Word'll spread.'

'Yep. Like wildfire.'

'That's Wirralong for you. Always good for a gossip.'

'Yeah, and this bloody business could get a whole lot worse before we're through.'

As they moved off, Jenna screwed her car's petrol cap back in place, her thoughts whirling. Clearly, there were more properties than Sam's involved in this fencing issue.

She'd only spent a short time in the district, but she'd learned enough to know that these farmers were already struggling with the drought. They didn't need the added burden of having their access to one of the few natural water sources fenced off.

But perhaps I should stop mulling over this and just get back to Melbourne, to my own mounting piles of work.

Wrestling with this, Jenna headed across the bitumen to pay for her petrol. She'd only reached halfway to the service station's shop, however, when the memory stirred.

Perhaps it was the hot sun beating down on her head, or the recent conversation about Cate's dad, but suddenly, against her will, Jenna was back in the past—the past she'd tried so hard to block out.

Oh, God. The threat of these harrowing memories was the very reason Jenna had stayed away from the outback, why she kept herself safely in the city. Safely busy, working long hours. But now, after just one weekend away from her urban refuge, the worst was happening.

She was back in another outback town, on another hot day, surrounded by dry, barren paddocks, and with the sun beating down …

AT TEN YEARS of age, Jenna had been old enough to recognise that her parents' worries were worse than ever. After months of extended drought, her mother and father seemed increasingly stressed and at night, when Jenna had lain awake pretending to be asleep, she'd listened to their anxious, sharp-voiced conversations in the kitchen.

She hadn't really understood the talk of banks and debt, of bills and foreclosures, but she'd known that the food served at their dinner table had been getting leaner and meaner and she'd guessed that her parents were running out of money. But she'd never dreamed …

Just thinking about it now, Jenna flinched and almost stumbled, but she couldn't hold back the other, worse memory … of her ten-year-old self arriving at the door to her father's huge corrugated iron, machinery shed.

She'd often visited him out there, spending hours perched on an oil drum and chatting happily, while he tinkered with the innards of a tractor or some other piece of machinery. She would tell her dad about school, about her friends, about Billy Jones's latest prank, or the book she was currently reading. Her dad wasn't a talkative man, but he'd always been happy to listen to her nattering, and to occasionally offer a nugget of advice or to give her a nod of approval.

He'd called Jenna his golden girl and she known that she occupied a special place in his heart—which made the memory all the more terrible.

On this day, it was the silence that Jenna noticed first. No tinkering of a spanner against metal, no gentle revving to coax an engine to life. As Jenna reached the shed's open doorway, she saw a shadow on the concrete floor. An elongated and exaggerated shape, but even so, a shape that was unbelievably, appallingly recognisable as the shadow of a figure dangling from a rope.

And then, in unbearable horror, Jenna had looked up.

Chapter Eight

THE GIRL AT the Wirralong Hotel's reception desk looked somewhat stunned when Jenna strode in.

'Hi, Dodie.' This time, Jenna made sure she checked the girl's name badge. 'I was wondering if you might have another room free?'

Dodie stopped gaping and flashed a bright smile. 'Right, Ms Matthews. Well, yes, sure.' She swivelled in her chair to study the computer screen. 'Are you looking for a booking for just one night?'

'Possibly,' said Jenna. 'But there's also a chance I might need to stay longer.'

'That's okay.' Dodie, having recovered from her surprise, was quite smooth and professional now, despite struggling to hide her curiosity. 'We're not heavily booked. In fact, I can offer you the same room that you had before, if you like.'

'Yes, that would be fine.' Jenna had noticed on her previous stay that the room in question had a desk and Wi-Fi, which was all she needed to set up a temporary office.

'Good-o. So, as you've been here before, you know about our dining room and the games room.'

'Yes, yes.' Jenna waved this aside. 'But I'm here on business, so I'll probably just eat in my room.'

Dodie's eyebrows rose to impossible heights. No doubt she was trying to reconcile Jenna's current 'business' with the city bridesmaid who'd spent a night at Sam Twist's grazing property on the dubious pretext of attending to newborn lambs.

'That's absolutely fine,' she said a shade too brightly as Jenna handed her a credit card. 'You'll find a Wi-Fi password and the menu for room service on the desk in your room.'

'Perfect.'

'Lovely to have you back so soon.'

'Thanks, Dodie.'

Carrying her overnight bag and laptop, Jenna climbed the grand old timber staircase rather than using the lift. If she stayed on, she would have to check if there was a gym in Wirralong.

Once inside the room, she drew the curtains, blocking the view of the town's main street, then switched on the aircon and opened her laptop. She also turned on her phone and watched a torrent of messages fill her screen.

Kicking off her shoes, she flopped into a comfy chair and scanned the messages. Amazingly, no one seemed to have thrown a tantrum or be panicking about her silence over the weekend. *Phew.* A big relief. And among the host of messages from colleagues and clients, she spotted one from Cate.

Just wanted to thank you again for being our beautiful

bridesmaid. Craig and I are now in Bali and it's heaven. Hope Sam is looking after you and that you're having almost as much fun as we are. C&C xx

Jenna smiled. The message had been sent yesterday and if she had responded then, while she was still in the grip of Sam Twist insta-lust, she might well have written an X-rated reply.

Today, however, Jenna was not only facing the overload of tasks relating to her usual work, but the problem of this fence and Sam's writ, plus the disturbing possibility that more innocent farmers in this region were affected.

Talk about coming back to reality with a thump. Worse—*oh, God*—Jenna was still gutted by the horrifying flashback to her father's suicide, the nightmare that forever haunted her dreams. But even as she'd struggled in that terrifying moment, besieged by those sickening memories, she had recognised a new challenge.

She'd understood with startling clarity that she couldn't just blithely drive away from Wirralong without a backward glance. It wasn't just Sam's problem that bothered her now. If there were other struggling graziers, like her father, who were battling bullies as well as the drought, she wanted to know about it.

Deep down, Jenna suspected that this was why she'd become a lawyer in the first place—to acquire the smarts to fight for the underdog. And now, no question—she needed to investigate this fencing issue further. If necessary, she would take the work on without the backup of her colleagues.

Not that she would mention any of these developments to Cate.

Brilliant weekend, she texted back. *But my news will keep.* She knew that such a noncommittal response would keep her friend guessing and desperately curious, but Cate would get over it. She was on her honeymoon after all. *So glad you're having a great time,* Jenna added. *Love to you and Craig. Xx*

JENNA WAITED TILL Tuesday night to ring Sam.

By then, she had put in more than thirty long, hard hours and, with the help of the necessary documents and files emailed through from Melbourne by her resourceful PA, she'd caught up on most of her work for clients. Perhaps, more importantly for Jenna, she'd made interesting discoveries about the fencing situation.

Now, as she pressed Sam's number on her phone, she was dismayed to feel her heart fluttering crazily. The phone rang and rang and she pictured him out in a paddock, or busy with the lambs, or even taking a shower. By the time he answered, she'd worked herself into quite a state of breathlessness.

'Hello?' Sam sounded ultra-cautious. No doubt he'd had oodles of phone calls from locals now that word had spread about his writ.

'Sam, it's me, Jenna.'

'Jenna!' The obvious pleasure in his voice was so unexpected she found herself grinning like a fool. 'Great to hear from you,' he said.

Such a surprise. Sam had been tense when she'd left Fenton and they'd both been very clear that, for both of them, this was goodbye. Jenna had half-expected he'd be evasive with her now.

'How are the lambs?' she asked, playing it cautious.

'Going great guns. Molly's guzzling so strongly now, I reckon I'll need to rename her.'

'Greedy Guts?'

'That would be appropriate.'

Jenna laughed. 'Great. I'm so pleased.'

'I'll tell her you called,' Sam added.

This brought another laugh and a poignant reminder of the many laughs she and Sam had shared in the short time they'd been together. It was also a reminder for Jenna that she hardly ever laughed in her everyday life, the life she'd guarded so carefully.

'Give her a cuddle from me,' she said.

'I'd rather give you a cuddle.'

Zap. Jenna had been relaxing on the bed, leaning back against the pillows, but as Sam's deep, seductive voice shot through her, this position seemed a very bad idea.

Abruptly, she rose from the bed and began to pace the

room. 'Have you heard from Michael Peterson?' she asked.

'Michael who?'

'Peterson. He's a legal colleague, the guy I mentioned who'd be perfect to help you with the writ.'

'Oh, yeah, right. I've been trying to forget about that.'

'Sam,' she reproached.

'And no, I haven't heard from him.'

'Well, I've spoken to him and he's keen, so you'll hear soon, I'm sure.'

'Can't wait,' Sam responded dryly. And Jenna might have scolded him again, but he added in a gentler tone, 'No, seriously, Jenna, thank you. It's very good of you to have bothered.'

Given his former hostility, this conciliatory response was most definitely a step in the right direction.

'No problem.' Jenna paused and found herself checking her reflection in the full-length mirror by the door, almost as if Sam could actually see her. At the same time, a clock on a monument outside in the main street began to chime the hour.

'Where are you?' asked Sam.

'I'm—' She was cautious about telling him she was still in the district. 'Why do you ask?'

'It's just that we have an old clock in Wirralong that sounds exactly like that.'

'Funny you should mention it.' Jenna tried to keep her voice light.

'Why? You're not in Wirralong?'

She supposed there was no point in lying. 'Yes, I am.'

'You've come back?'

'I never actually left. I stayed on, Sam. I wanted to check out this situation with the fence. There are more farmers than you involved.'

'Yes, but—' Sam stopped, clearly stumped. 'What are you doing exactly? What are you planning?'

'I don't have a clear plan yet. I'm investigating. It's still early days.' Jenna was about to add more about her discoveries, when Sam distracted her.

'Where are you staying?' he asked.

'In town.'

'The pub in Main Street? The Wirralong Hotel?'

'Ah …' What the hell. 'Yep, that's the one.'

A small silence fell as he digested this. 'You might as well have stayed here.'

Jenna closed her eyes, which was a mistake, as it only served to intensify the flood of sweet memories. Of staying at Fenton. Of Sam's lips, his hands, his sensational body. Of sharing meals with him, caring for his lambs and travelling over his property. The crazy mix of excitement and contentment that had enveloped her all weekend.

'You know that's not a good idea, Sam.'

Another stretch of silence followed, while Jenna played with a fantasy of going back to Fenton and spending another night with him. She was seriously tempted to retract her last comment.

But then he spoke. 'Okay. Good luck with your investigations,' he said simply, and promptly hung up.

JENNA STOOD FOR ages, staring at the phone in her hand. She told herself she was an idiot to feel so let down. She had stayed in Wirralong because of the fence, not Sam. Sure, her weekend with him had been very pleasant—okay, quite possibly, a once in a lifetime, amazingly blissful and unforgettable experience.

But it was only ever meant to be a one-night stand. The extra night's extension had been an error of judgement.

And now, although she'd intended to discuss a few of the broader issues regarding the fence with Sam, she knew that staying at a clear distance from him was not only sensible, but important. Vital, in fact. They both needed to get back to their normal lives as quickly as possible. And, clearly, Sam agreed.

Good. *Get over yourself, Jenna.*

She checked her emails again, wrote thoughtful answers to two of them, then rang room service and ordered a bowl of Thai soup. Closing her laptop, she pushed it aside to make room to eat at her desk. From experience, she knew the kitchen staff in this pub weren't super-fast, so she decided to grab a quick shower before the soup arrived.

This evening, however, they were a little quicker than expected. Jenna had just emerged from the bathroom in a bathrobe and with her damp hair wrapped in a towel when she heard the knock on the door.

Tightening the knot on her robe's belt, she went to answer it.

'Good evening.'

Bloody hell.

Instead of the boy from the kitchen bearing a bowl of Tom Yum soup, Sam Twist filled Jenna's doorway.

'For God's sake, Sam.'

He must have broken all the speed limits to get here so quickly. He also looked all kinds of gorgeous as he stood there in pale chinos and a lemon, open-necked shirt.

'I know I should have warned you.'

'Of course you should have.'

'I was afraid you'd tell me to get lost.'

'And that was a very accurate assumption.' Jenna mustered as much dignity as she could manage, given her state of undress and the fact that her heart was thumping and her knees shaking, not to mention that her hair was dripping down the back of her neck.

Sam showed no sign of budging. 'Have you had dinner?'

She'd spent the past twenty minutes clearing her head of this guy and she was about to tell him that indeed she had already dined, thank you very much. But at that very moment the lift pinged and the doors slid open to reveal the kitchen boy coming down the hallway, bearing a tray with her bowl of soup.

'Here's my dinner right now,' she said haughtily.

Sam turned, gave the boy a polite nod and stepped back to allow him access to Jenna's room.

'Thanks so much,' she said to the boy and she smiled extra graciously, as he set the tray on her desk. Then she turned to Sam who had remained firmly in her doorway, narrowing her eyes in her best attempt at a 'get lost' glare.

His response was a smile and a quick foot in the door, just as soon as the kitchen boy departed. 'Jenna,' he said smoothly. 'Give me a moment.'

Sam didn't need another moment. They'd spoken on the phone just a few minutes ago.

'I'm sorry. I'd like to eat this before it gets cold.' With an overly dramatic, grand gesture, Jenna crossed the room and lifted the metal cover on her soup.

'That's your dinner?' Sam, who had followed her, sounded amused, as well as surprised, and Jenna had to admit the bowl did look rather smaller than she'd expectedentrée-sized at best.

'It's all I need,' she said stoutly.

'I promise you, Janu's can do better.'

'Janu's?'

'The five-hat restaurant just down the street and a favourite with the locals, including our winemakers.' Folding his arms across his considerable chest, Sam regarded her with a charming yet sceptical smile. 'It's only a few doors away. Haven't you seen it?'

'I've—I've been busy.' In truth, apart from an early morning jog, she'd hardly left the room.

'Jenna,' Sam said in mock dismay. 'I can't in all conscience leave you here in this room to eat a thimbleful of soup when I've booked a table for two at the best restaurant in town.'

She made a point of rolling her eyes. 'What are you trying to do, Sam? Our original agreement was a casual, no-strings, one-night stand. We've already broken that agreement and now you're trying to stretch it to a *third* night?'

She was pleased she'd managed to sound aggrieved, while ignoring the pesky voice in her head that whispered how intensely pleasurable a third night might be.

Sam, however, remained annoyingly unruffled. 'I'm asking you to have dinner with me, Jenna. Not to spend the night.'

'Oh.' Talk about being caught wrong-footed. 'Right, well—' She wanted to pout, to freeze Sam with her best death stare.

Instead, she took a very deep breath and refused to meet his gaze. The last thing she needed now was another glimpse of his amused, teasing smile.

'I really am sorry,' he added with a surprising note of contrition. 'I know I should have given you fair warning, and I didn't mean to barge in and derail your evening.' He sent another glance at her bowl of soup. 'I guess I was so surprised when I discovered you were still in town, I just raced in here on impulse.'

He had the grace to look embarrassed now. 'I must admit, that's not my normal MO. As I warned you at the start, you're bewitching, Jenna.'

Heat rushed into her cheeks and she almost weakened, almost admitted that he'd made a damned strong impression on her, as well. Somehow she found the strength to hold firm. 'Don't try to flatter me.'

No longer smiling, Sam looked again at the cooling, tiny bowl of soup. 'I'll leave you to it then.'

The wave of disappointment that swamped her was too ridiculous for words. Jenna hoped the sense of letdown didn't show in her face as Sam backed towards the door.

With his hand on the doorknob, he paused. 'I'll have to find out about your insights into the fencing issue some other time.'

Oh, God, the fence.

As Sam closed the door and departed, Jenna felt as if she'd been struck by lightning. Of course he'd come to find out more about the fence. He might have flattered her with talk of bewitching, but his stock and his property were his highest priorities. And how the hell could she have forgotten the sole reason she'd stayed on in Wirralong?

How could spending five minutes in the same room with the man have deleted her brain of basic common sense?

Yikes. The whole time Sam had been here, she'd been thinking of sex. And now she felt several versions of foolish as she opened the door again.

He was already at the lift.

'Sam?' she called.

As he turned to her, the lift pinged and the doors slid open.

Conscious that he was now holding the doors ajar and that she was out in the hallway in her bathrobe and with a towel around her head, Jenna spoke rapidly. 'Can you hang on a moment? I—I *would* like to discuss the fencing issue. To fill you in on what I've learned so far.'

Sam's only response was a slight dip of his head.

'If you could give me a few minutes to get dressed,' she said.

His eyebrows rose. 'So you'll come to dinner?'

Jenna gave a quick nod before retreating.

Chapter Nine

WHAT THE HELL was I thinking?

As Sam paced the pavement outside the Wirralong pub, he'd never felt quite so sideswiped or stunned, so bemused by his own behaviour.

He wasn't a man who lost his head over a woman. He was always interested, sure, very interested at times, but he played it cool. Always. If anything, he liked to let the women do the chasing. He'd certainly never dropped everything on the strength of one phone call and bolted into town like a desperate junkie needing a fix.

This evening's impulse was way out of line, but Sam had been staggered to realise that Jenna was still in Wirralong. Last he'd seen of her, she'd been dead-set desperate to race back to the city and her high-powered job. The fact that she'd stayed on to investigate the fencing left him gobsmacked.

And then, one glimpse of her in that damned bathrobe, her skin all softly pink and glowing from the shower, and his remaining brain cells had lost all capacity for rational thought. Served him right that Jenna had sent him packing.

Sam knew he'd done nothing to earn a last-minute reprieve in the form of her acceptance of his dinner invitation. But he was grateful, not least because he'd pleaded with his mate, the head chef at Janu's, to wangle him an eleventh-hour table for two. The restaurant's fame had spread far and wide, so even on a Tuesday night it was full, but now, against all odds, Sam had secured a booking and Jenna would be dining with him after all.

He'd told her not to rush. He could wait as long as she needed. In truth, it was he who needed time—to calm down, to get his head together, to drag his brains from below his belt.

This was to be a business dinner—dinner with a lawyer to discuss the serious issue of the fence and the writ. Sam had received enough phone calls over the past two days to know that half the district was fired up about having their access to the river cut off.

And if Jenna Matthews was willing to bring her legal expertise to the party, Sam owed it to his fellow graziers to pay attention. To pay attention to Jenna's advice and not to her clever green eyes, brimming with secrets and sex appeal. Nor to her sweet mouth, or her slim, beguiling curves, or the X-rated memories the sight of them evoked.

Committed focus on the issues at hand was Sam's plan for this evening. A man could only do his best.

JENNA TOLD HERSELF she shouldn't worry too much about her appearance for this dinner date, especially as it wasn't so much a date as a business meeting.

The only outfit she had with her that was even remotely suitable for a high-end restaurant was the dress she'd worn to work on the previous Friday. A slim-fitting, grey linen shift with a square cut neckline, it was actually one of her favourites, so that was a bonus. And her hair, already half-dry by the time Sam left, had insisted on keeping the natural waves she usually tried hard to disguise.

Finally, for some reason she couldn't quite explain, Jenna found herself applying her makeup with the ease and skill of a professional. She had to blink when she saw the results in the mirror. *Wow.* She hoped she didn't look as if she'd tried too hard, but it was too late to start over.

A crazy fluttering began in her chest as she took the lift downstairs. She tried for deep, calming breaths and reminded herself that she was only here to help farmers like her dad, who were struggling with the drought. The fact that one of these farmers was Sam Twist was beside the point.

Until the lift doors slid open and she saw him standing in the hotel lobby.

Damn it, the man was hot. Panty-dropping hot.

Stop it, Jenna. Behave yourself.

It didn't help that Sam was looking at her as if he wanted to eat her.

'Hey there,' he said, but he was no longer smiling and he

didn't look particularly relaxed, or confident either.

Jenna wasn't sure what to make of that.

'Have a great evening!' called a voice from behind them and Jenna turned to see Dodie grinning like a Cheshire cat. Didn't that girl ever take time off?

WIRRALONG'S BEST RESTAURANT was seriously impressive. Jenna's assumptions about country dining had mostly involved a hamburger with the works in a grimy roadhouse. Janu's, however, was most definitely high end, with gleaming, polished floorboards, exposed brick walls, a stainless-steel bar and an air of quiet sophistication that would have been at home in any metropolitan setting.

'Wow!' she said. 'This is stunning, Sam.'

He looked pleased and seemed to relax a little as they were shown to a table in a corner that proved surprisingly private, despite the fact that the restaurant was full.

'You must have been lucky to get a booking,' she added.

'I was. It helps to have connections in the kitchen.'

'Lucky you—and lucky me, too, on this occasion.' Jenna smiled, but she made a conscious decision to put a halt on smiling. If she wasn't careful, she would spend the entire evening sending drippy grins across the table.

A waiter filled their crystal water glasses and offered a wine list, which she paid studious attention to.

'What do you fancy?' Sam asked her.

'What do you recommend?'

'Quite a few of these wines are grown and produced locally.'

'Yes, I tried a red at your place. It was great.'

'Would you like another? Or would you prefer something from Europe?'

'Oh, let's stay local. Low food miles.'

Sam gave a smiling nod. 'Another red then? Perhaps a shiraz?'

'Sounds great.'

Jenna was very used to dining with clients, but she wasn't in the habit of sleeping with them and, this evening, despite the business that needed to be discussed, she found the simple process of choosing wine and musing over the menu infused with high-octane sparks.

Annoyingly, she had to keep reminding herself to settle down, to keep her focus on business. The fence. The river. The farmers.

Their wine arrived, served by a discreet waiter and poured into massive, shining glasses, which Jenna and Sam clinked together carefully.

'Cheers,' Sam said. 'Here's to a happy stay in Wirralong.'

'Thanks. And here's to a successful outcome.'

The wine was ruby red, peppery and mellow. Superb, and no doubt very expensive. Aware that she shouldn't become too relaxed, Jenna set her glass down after the initial sip.

'So, about the fence and the river,' she said.

Sam nodded and his eyes were instantly alert.

'As I'm sure you must know, graziers would normally have riparian rights.'

'Allowing access to the river?' He frowned. 'Of course we do. Why do you think I cut the fence?'

Jenna smiled. 'And you'd normally be able to argue that your rights had been infringed when this fence was erected. But you've been served a writ through the courts, and that wouldn't have happened if Thorsborne Holdings, the mining company in question, hadn't been given authority to put that fence up.'

'Authority? You mean they have an authority to fence that's separate from their authority to prospect?'

'That's exactly what I mean.'

Sam sank back in his chair, clearly appalled. 'But that's ridiculous.'

'It's unusual.'

'Thorsborne Holdings already have exclusive rights to prospect everything from bloody gold and silver to rare earth. And now you're saying they also have authority to fence off twenty-five kilometres of the bloody river—of *our* river?'

'I'm afraid so, Sam.'

'No way.' He gave a savage shake of his head. 'They snuck in and put those fences up virtually overnight. That's got to be dodgy.'

'You would think so,' Jenna agreed. 'But I've been making enquiries, and it seems the new State Minister for Mining has ticked off on the project. It's been more or less kept under wraps, and it certainly didn't get much coverage in the press, but apparently he's claiming the project is a major benefit to the community.'

'Like hell it is.'

'And the fence is necessary for security and public safety.'

Sam looked fit to explode. '*That*,' he said with fierce emphasis, 'is a *total* load of bullshit.'

Just as well their table was some distance from other diners.

'I know it's infuriating, Sam, but as far as I can see, Thorsborne Holdings have managed to wangle a lease agreement with the state that overrides your right to access the water.'

'Fuck.' The expletive was dropped on a note of quiet desperation.

'It's going to be a hard one to fight,' Jenna admitted. 'An international mining company like Thorsborne has scads of money and legal muscle. If you tried to take them on, it could cost a huge amount and drag on for years.'

'So, what are you saying?' His eyes glittered with fury. 'We should simply give in?'

'No,' Jenna said, just as their meals arrived.

'For you, madam.' The waiter placed a roasted pumpkin salad with salami, chickpeas and garlic-buttered brussels sprouts in front of Jenna.

'Thank you,' she said. 'That looks amazing.'

'And for you, sir.'

Sam had opted for grilled pork chops with plums, halloumi and lemon, which looked equally sensational. He nodded his thanks to the waiter, then sat with poorly contained patience while the fellow, with exquisite care, topped up their wine glasses.

At last the waiter melted away and Sam fixed his gaze on Jenna. 'Sounds like you're telling me it's dead easy for Thorsborne to push the local graziers around and we haven't got a hope in hell.'

'I'm still looking into it, Sam. I don't think the case is completely hopeless. It does seem short-sighted of the state government to allow Thorsborne to charge in the way they have, with absolutely no consideration for the rights of the adjacent landholders to water their stock.'

'But is that a strong enough argument?'

Jenna gave a cautious nod. 'Handled correctly, it could be, yes.'

His eyes widened.

'I can't promise,' Jenna added.

'But you're really prepared to help?'

'Let's say I'm looking into it. I need to do more research—to talk to my colleagues—but I'd certainly like to help, if I can.'

Sam regarded her with a look of smiling disbelief. 'But

that's great. It's incredible, Jenna. I—I—' He seemed at a loss for words.

I know, she almost told him. She couldn't quite believe the way this case had so easily gripped her either. She'd never thought of herself as any kind of crusader.

Just then, Sam seemed to remember their meals and his role as host. 'Please,' he said with a gentlemanly gesture towards her plate. 'Enjoy your meal.'

'I will. It looks so good.' Picking up her fork, Jenna speared a brussels sprout and took a bite. The garlic and butter blended perfectly with the vegetable's roasted nutty crunch. 'Mmm. I'm in heaven.' She took a deep sip of her wine and allowed herself a smile. 'Your meal looks great too.'

'Yeah. Brad runs a great show here.'

They settled to eating. Jenna realised she was ravenous and the food was truly delicious. She took several more sips of wine. Medium-bodied and elegant, it was a perfect accompaniment to the subtle flavours on her plate.

Sam had just sliced a golden brown chunk of halloumi when he looked up, his grey eyes serious for once, rather than teasing. 'Can I ask why?'

'Why …?'

'I know you're a busy city lawyer, Jenna. Cate's told me about the long hours you work. Why would you want to be distracted by something like this?'

She wasn't prepared to tell Sam about the promptings from her family history. That was a story she never discussed.

She smiled carefully. 'Don't take this the wrong way, but I discovered there were more folk than just you involved in this. People in this district who might be even more vulnerable. Graziers, like Cate's dad.'

'Ted Jeffries?'

'Yes.'

Sam acknowledged this with a thoughtful nod, and his smile, as he regarded her, was thoughtful, too. He seemed about to say something more when a stranger approached their table, a man around Sam's age, impressively tall and broad shouldered.

'Evening, Sam.'

'Cameron,' Sam responded warmly. 'How are you?'

'Couldn't be better.' The man nodded towards Jenna and smiled.

'Jenna,' said Sam. 'Let me introduce our local copper, Cameron James. Cameron, Jenna Matthews.'

The policeman nodded. 'Pleased to meet you, Jenna.'

'You, too, Sergeant.'

Still smiling, Cameron James eyed her shrewdly for a moment, then his expression sobered as he quickly turned back to Sam, who was clearly the reason he'd stopped.

'I hear you've had a visitor from the courts,' he said.

'Yep, but it's all in hand.'

The policeman waited a moment, as if he expected Sam to expand on this. When Sam remained silent, he leaned closer, lowering his voice, but Jenna could catch his words.

'Be careful, mate. Seems you've started a rebellion.'

Sam frowned. 'A rebellion?'

'Old Jeffries has cut his fence too.'

Jenna's gasp was an echo of Sam's. She thought again of Cate's father, with his gentle, proud smile as he escorted his daughter on her wedding day. Of Cate, now blissfully unaware, enjoying her honeymoon in Bali, of the shock her friend would receive if she came home and found her father in trouble with the law.

'When did this happen?' Sam asked.

'Late this afternoon, I believe.' The policeman laid a strong hand on Sam's shoulder, gave him a matey pat and then straightened. 'Just take care, won't you? Remember, this mining mob's bound to have a lot of fire power.' With a nod of farewell, he walked on.

From across the table, Jenna watched Sam let out a huff of breath. She'd never seen him look quite so grim. 'Did you know about this?' he asked her.

'No,' she said. 'I knew Ted Jeffries was upset about the fence and I knew he'd been talking to others around Wirralong, but I had no idea he would cut his fence, too.'

'You can't blame him for getting stirred up.'

'You can't, no, and maybe your copper mate's right about a rebellion.'

'Jeez, I hope not. But yeah, maybe.' Sam sighed again, then picked up his wine glass and sent her a cheeky smile, an echo of the confident, almost cocky best man she'd met just a few nights ago. 'Just as well we have you on our case,' he said, raising his glass to her.

Jenna wished she felt more certain that she really could help.

Chapter Ten

A S THEY LEFT the restaurant, a cool breeze whispered along Wirralong's main street. Jenna, in a sleeveless summer dress, shivered and Sam couldn't resist putting his arm around her. To keep her warm, of course, although he couldn't deny that he'd been distracted by her lovely bare shoulders all evening, just as he'd been when she'd first snagged his attention in her bridesmaid's gown.

He half expected Jenna to shrug away from him. He knew she was as keen as he was to keep their wild weekend at fling status. But she let his arm stay there as she walked in silence, with her own arms folded across her chest, her head bowed, apparently deep in thought.

'I should talk to Cate's dad before I leave,' she said, after a bit.

It was the first time this evening that Jenna had mentioned leaving and Sam tried to ignore the prickle of disquiet. Of course she wouldn't hang around any longer than was absolutely necessary. 'Would you phone Ted for a chat, or go out to his place?' he asked.

'I think I should go out there. It would be better if I

spoke to him face to face. I don't want to alarm him, but I think I should warn him that, potentially, he could find himself with a writ, too. It might help if I explain that I'm looking into legal options.'

Jenna seemed anxious as she said this. She was Cate's friend, so Sam supposed it made sense that she was concerned for old Ted Jeffries. But he couldn't shake off the feeling that there was something else, something deeper at the heart of her interest in this case. It was almost as if the hotshot city lawyer actually understood the emotional anguish that so often gripped people on the land—the helplessness of being at the mercy of unpredictable weather and markets and politicians who only pretended to care.

Perhaps she simply liked the idea of defending battlers?

That thought warmed Sam more than it should have.

'You're not thinking of going out to Ted's place tonight?' he asked.

'No, not tonight. I'm sure it's too late now. First thing in the morning, perhaps.'

'Would you like me to come with you?' The offer was out before he'd properly thought it through.

'That would be wonderful. I'm sure Ted would be much more relaxed if you were there.' Jenna turned to him then and gave him one of her radiantly beautiful smiles.

And Sam couldn't help himself. He kissed her. Just a kiss on her cheek at first, but she didn't pull away and so he drew her closer and found her lips, soft and warm and yielding to him.

A soft groan broke from him and, damn it, he didn't care that he was in Wirralong's main street. Slipping his arms around her, he pulled her hard against him and kissed her deeply. Kissed her with his eyes closed, losing himself in the mind-blowing pleasure of her sweet mouth, of her soft curves pressing into him just so, in the dizzying, intoxicating marvel that was Jenna.

And she didn't seem to mind, although she couldn't let him get away without a reprimand when she eventually stepped out of his embrace.

'That wasn't supposed to happen,' she said, looking pink and flushed.

He chanced a small smile. 'I hope you don't expect me to apologise.'

'No. I suspect apologies aren't your strong suit.' Her arched-eyebrow glance told him she had his measure.

By now, they had reached the hotel and Sam was pleased there was no one at the reception desk, although he knew the stories about them would already be rife. Young Dodie Gulliver was one of the town's keenest gossips.

In the doorway, Jenna said, 'Thanks for a lovely dinner.'

'My pleasure.'

Lifting her neat little chin to a haughty angle, she added, 'I'll see you in the morning then.' Her tone was businesslike now, no doubt a warning to keep his distance 'What time suits you?'

'I don't mind.' With a bit of juggling, he could still manage his usual morning routine. 'Would nine be okay?'

Jenna nodded. 'Of course.'

'I'll ring Ted if you like, just to let him know we're coming.'

'I'd appreciate that. Thanks.'

Sam didn't try to kiss her again, despite a crazy, raging fantasy that involved Jenna inviting him up to her room.

He took a step back. 'Goodnight, Jenna.'

'Goodnight.'

For a fleeting moment, she looked vulnerable and so breath-robbing beautiful Sam almost weakened and went in for another kiss. But then she straightened her shoulders, performed a smart about turn, and headed for the lift.

He left without looking back.

THE JEFFRIES' PROPERTY was in a similarly parched and sad state to Fenton, but the house and its surrounds were considerably more downtrodden. The homestead exterior had peeling paint, broken guttering and sagging verandahs, plus the remnants of a garden that was now more weeds than anything. Jenna supposed gardening might have been Cate's mother's domain.

And Ted, when he met Jenna and Sam at the front door, looked like he'd aged an extra ten years. The house was dusty inside, the windows grimy. Clearly, Cate's brothers didn't help much with housework.

Ted took Jenna and Sam through to a seventies-style kitchen with orange bench tops and shabby mission brown cupboards, where he had a pot of tea already made, and mugs ready with a packet of Anzac biscuits.

A little necessary small talk followed, as they took their seats at the kitchen table and Ted poured their tea and asked about sugar and milk. They chatted about the wedding and about Cate and Craig on their honeymoon.

Jenna showed Ted a photo on her phone that Cate had sent, a selfie with Craig beneath a palm tree, showing a backdrop of white sandy beach and glittering blue sea. Cate was wearing a lavender bikini with a beautiful aqua and purple sari, stylishly tied around her hips.

Ted smiled fondly. 'She looks very happy, doesn't she?'

'She looks amazing,' Jenna replied warmly. 'And yes, happy, too. I think Craig makes her very happy indeed.'

Ted nodded. 'And I'm looking forward to having her close by again.'

'I'm sure you must be.' But then, out of the blue, Jenna found her thoughts zapping to her own father, imagining that he too had reached Ted's age. She pictured him, white haired and possibly arthritic, his skin brown and leathery from years of living on the land. She could even picture her dad looking forward to seeing her when she came to visit him, his arms open wide to hug her.

Oh, God. It was only when she felt the stinging in her throat and eyes that she realised how dangerously carried away she'd been. And then she caught Sam watching her with a concerned frown.

Yikes, he couldn't have guessed, but he must be wondering …

It was time to get a grip.

'Anyhow, the way things are going around here—' Ted, fortunately, hadn't noticed Jenna's lapse, and had continued talking. Now he sighed and left his sentence dangling, as he ran a thin, knobbly hand through the straggling remains of his fine white hair. 'The last thing this district needs is those mining bastards and their bloody fence.' He winced. 'Sorry about the language, Jenna.'

'Don't worry,' said Sam. 'Jenna's used to hearing me sound off about Thorsborne.'

'It's hard,' Jenna agreed as she set a pad and pen on the table. 'If you don't mind, Ted, I'd like to take a few notes—about your thoughts on this situation and your circumstances—and why you felt you had to cut the fence.'

His shaggy white eyebrows rose, making deep wrinkles in his sun-browned forehead. 'You really think it will help? You can't stop them, can you?'

'I'm hoping we can get this ruling overturned.'

'Through the courts?'

'Yes.'

'Against a huge mining company? It'll cost a fortune.'

'I can't make promises, Ted, but I'm certainly looking into the best options.'

He sat for a moment, looking uncertain, almost disbelieving, but then his mouth tilted in a crooked smile. 'Good for you, lass. I wish you all the very best.'

SAM WAS QUIET as he drove Jenna back into town, but that suited her. It meant she could check the messages on her phone, even answering one or two of the most urgent.

She also fielded a phone call from one of her most important clients, assuring him that her PA would send all the relevant documentation through for his signature within the hour.

It was only as the call ended that she realised Sam was pulling off the road and into parkland on the outskirts of Wirralong township.

'Why are you stopping?' she asked as he came to a halt in the shade of a huge, lemon-scented gum.

The park was empty and quiet. Picnic tables and barbecues were scattered about, as well as play equipment for kids, but it was a week day, so the kids were in school and there were no other parked cars or people in sight.

Sam unclipped his seat belt and shifted in his seat, as if making himself more comfortable. He didn't speak at first and from the tree overhead, a pair of kookaburras filled the silence with a burst of cackling laughter. Jenna, suddenly tense, thought they sounded demented.

'What is it, Sam?' He was making her quite uneasy. 'Why have you stopped?'

His face twisted in a grimace. 'I'm trying to work out how to put this.'

Jenna's edginess deepened. 'Put what?'

'The thing that's bothering me.'

'About the case?'

'About you, Jenna.'

Heat flared in her face. What had she done? Was he about to tell her to butt out of this Thorsborne business? To insist that the locals of Wirralong could manage on their own, thank you very much?

'If you think I'm interfering—'

'It's not that.' Frowning, Sam tapped a tattoo on the steering wheel, obviously wrestling to find the right words. 'I don't think you're interfering and I'm really grateful that you care about the issues of a small country town. I suppose that's what I'd like to understand,' he said. 'I mean, you're on the phone every chance you get, obviously flat out with your city work.'

'Well—yes.'

'But this morning, when you were talking with Ted, you looked genuinely upset, and for a moment there, it was almost as if—' Sam paused, then slapped the steering wheel with an open palm. 'Jeez, Jenna, I don't know where I'm going with this. But there was this look in your eyes that got me in the gut. I knew there was something deeper going on.'

Jenna sat very still, not sure what to say.

'I realised I know hardly anything about you. Almost nothing about your people—your family.'

Whack. The blow landed far too close for comfort. Jenna didn't talk about her family. She'd always deemed it safer not to start down that track. Now she wished she could think of something to say, something innocuous, anything to buy herself some thinking time.

But Sam was persistent. 'I seem to remember you told me you have a mother and sister in Brisbane?'

She nodded. She supposed she could talk about Sally and her mum with a certain degree of safety, and perhaps that would keep Sam happy. 'My sister, Sally, is married with two kids—a boy and a girl,' she said. 'Sal's husband is a plumber and she's a school teacher. At Ashgrove Primary. I guess she's following in our mother's footsteps. Mum was a teacher's aide for years and years until she retired.'

'So you've no other lawyers in the family?'

'God no. Mum and Sal have more sense.' Jenna noticed Sam didn't smile at this weak joke. 'And I'm not saying that to badmouth my own profession,' she added. 'It's just that I think they made the right choices. They're very happy.'

Jenna had watched her mother begin to heal almost as soon as she'd arrived in the city. Alice Matthews had thrived in the steady, reliable and wonderfully ordinary world of suburban Brisbane primary schools. Sally had recognised this too and she was as contented with her work and her nice little family as anyone Jenna knew.

'And your father?' Sam asked, slipping the question in neatly.

Jenna swallowed hard, snatched a quick breath. 'He died when I was ten.' *Please, Sam, drop this now.*

'I'm sorry,' Sam said. 'That must have been hard on all of you. Were you in Brisbane then?'

Jenna almost didn't answer, but she guessed that if she tried to avoid this, her silence would only add to Sam's curiosity. Which wouldn't matter so much, if she was never going to see him again, but she'd nixed that possibility when she voiced her commitment to the Thorsborne case.

It didn't help that Sam was asking out of genuine concern. And Jenna realised she'd let her guard down when she talked so easily about her mum and Sally. Now, the only sensible option was to share with Sam the awful truth.

'Not Brisbane,' she said softly. 'My dad died in Boulia.'

'Boulia?' Sam sounded quite shocked. 'In far western Queensland?'

'Yes.'

'That's a bloody long way out. Almost desert country. You weren't living there, too, were you?'

Jenna knew he was watching her, waiting. She felt as tense as a hair-trigger on a gun as she nodded.

'Were you on the land?' he asked.

'My parents had cattle. And a few sheep.'

'Molly, the lamb?'

Again she gave a nod. 'Yep.'

To her dismay, the word came on a sob and with that, welling emotions took hold and the unravelling began. Her mouth pulled out of shape and her lips trembled.

'Jenna, what is it? Hell. I'm sorry. What's the matter?'

She didn't want to tell him. Didn't want to. Didn't want to. But in the end, the words just tumbled out.

'There was a drought. A really terrible one that went on for years. Then there was money trouble, of course, and pressure from the banks, and it obviously got too much—for my father.'

'Oh, Jenna. Not suicide?'

'Yes.' The single syllable erupted in a squeak.

'And you were only ten. Jesus.'

'I was the one who found him. Out in the shed.'

'Oh, God.'

Tears were already dripping down Jenna's cheeks, but now she exploded into noisy weeping.

'Jen, I'm so sorry.'

She shook her head, unable to speak and the tears fell in a flood now, accompanied by embarrassingly loud sobs. She was helpless to stop any of it and only dimly aware that Sam had unclipped her seat belt and had somehow moved closer, drawing her into his arms.

She was too deeply sunk in the agony of her loss, in the

horror of remembering that moment when she'd found her father in the shed, in the terror of racing back to her mother, speechless with shock, in the ordeal of the ghastly weeks that had followed.

In the pain that had never, ever gone away.

'Jenna,' Sam soothed.

He was holding her, rocking her gently, but it was some time before the onslaught of devastation finally began to ease.

Over the years, Jenna had come to recognise the pattern of her grief, arriving in an overwhelming tidal wave of pain and loss that eventually retreated like the ebbing of a dark sea. She knew she would never be free of this, but now as she emerged from darkness into the everyday world of a roadside park on the outskirts of Wirralong, she also realised she'd been weeping her heart out on Sam Twist's shoulder.

'Sorry,' she said, lifting her tear-stained face. 'I hope I haven't made your shirt all wet.'

'As if that matters.'

'But I'm so sorry for crying all over you.'

'It's okay, Jenna. Hell—that's a huge thing to carry.'

She swallowed another threatening sob. 'That's why I try not to talk about it.'

'Yeah, it must be hard. I shouldn't have—'

The poor guy sounded as if he was struggling, as if he felt out of his depth. No doubt he was wishing he could be anywhere except trapped in a car with a wailing woman.

'I'm just so sorry,' he said.

'You've been very sweet, Sam. Thanks.'

He hugged her gently and she drew another ragged breath, grateful that the worst was over. It was only then that she became aware of the reassuring warmth and strength of Sam's arms around her, and she inhaled the clean woodsy scent of his skin.

He dropped the sweetest of kisses on her damp cheek, another on her chin, and yet another on the tip of her nose, which she knew must be bright red and shiny from her crying.

In that moment, she realised she'd never felt quite so comforted by another person, certainly not by a man. Which was quite a revelation, given that this was the same man who, just a few nights ago, had also awoken her inner sex maniac.

Now, with Sam still holding her close, and with the weight of her sorrow easing in her chest, she wound her arms tightly around him in grateful thanks, and her heart seemed to lift like a bird taking flight. She wondered if it was possible to just keep on flying, floating on a cloud of perfect peace and quiet, of fragile, inexplicable calm.

Chapter Eleven

S AM COULDN'T QUITE believe he was actually okay with holding a weeping woman in his arms. Not just okay but totally sympathetic, rather than wishing he could escape.

Just the same, he felt lousy about pushing Jenna into telling her story. Now the mystery of her interest in this Thorsborne case was solved, but in doing so he'd caused her all this pain and something heavy, like a boulder, had lodged in his throat.

He wished he could think of the rights words to say, but he was a sheep farmer, not a psychologist. It was almost impossible to offer helpful words about such a shitty situation. He ran the risk of sounding like a Hallmark card.

As he'd held Jenna, he'd found himself thinking of his own dad's death and how gutted he'd been. And that was despite the fact that his dad had been given all kinds of medical and emotional support and his mum had been downright courageous in her role as his nurse and carer.

His dad had put up a tough battle to the end. Even so, his death had been devastating. Sam couldn't imagine what it would be like to lose a parent through suicide.

And Jenna had been so young when she'd witnessed that terrible sight. Surely, it would be burnt into her soul and haunt her for the rest of her life.

The poor kid.

No wonder, though, that she cared about old Ted Jeffries. He wasn't just her best friend's dad. He was another vulnerable grazier. On the brink.

Now, as Jenna edged out of his arms, she found a tissue in her carry bag and gave her nose a good blow. 'Phew!' she said. 'I'm glad that's behind us.'

'At least you're one of only a small group of women who still look beautiful when they cry.' It was true. Jenna did manage to look surprisingly delightful with her golden hair a messy tangle and her eyes and nose pink.

'Liar,' she said. 'Or perhaps you make women cry on a regular basis, so you're some kind of expert?'

'Okay, I deserved that.'

'No, you didn't.' Jenna offered him a small smile. 'You've been lovely, Sam.' Leaning closer, she kissed him on the jaw. 'Thanks for looking after me. You couldn't have been nicer.'

'Nicer, huh?' There was nothing 'nice' about Sam's rampaging thoughts as her soft lips lingered along his jawline. In fact, if it hadn't been broad daylight, he might have revised his attitude to sexual gymnastics in bucket car seats. Except that it would be crassness of the highest order, especially given Jenna's emotional state.

'Anyway,' Jenna said as she dumped the damp tissue back into her bag, 'I'm sure you need to get back to Fenton and I should be getting back to Melbourne.'

Sam blinked at this sudden about turn. 'Now? Today?'

'Yes. I think I've done as much here as I can for the time being.'

'I see. Yes, sure.'

'I've already checked out of the hotel.' Jenna tucked stray, curling strands of hair behind her ear. 'My car is packed and ready for take-off.'

This made total sense, so why hadn't he expected it? Surely a few minutes of holding Jenna in his arms while she wept on his shoulder weren't enough to throw him right off track?

'I need to talk to my colleagues and plan a few strategies,' she said.

'Of course.'

'But I'll stay in touch, Sam,' she added, making him wonder if his bizarre reaction of disappointment had shown in his face. 'I promise I'll keep the ball rolling. You don't have to worry that I'll drop this case, as soon as I'm out of town.'

'I wasn't thinking anything of the sort.'

'Good.' Already, Jenna was re-buckling her seat belt.

Sam followed suit and gunned the motor. With deliberate effort, he cleared his head of sensory clutter—the flowery scent of Jenna's hair, the petal-soft seduction of her lips on his jaw, her vulnerability as she'd clung to him while she wept.

Easing off the handbrake, he steered out of the shady park and into the blazing sunlight of the main road into town. Scant minutes later, he was pulling up in the car park behind the hotel, just a few parking spots away from Jenna's neat little peacock-blue sedan.

They both got out, Jenna with her sunglasses now in place, her carry bag hitched over one shoulder and her car keys in hand. In the sunlight her hair was spun gold.

'So, this is goodbye,' she said, with a grim little smile.

'Let's make it *see you later*.'

'Yes, of course.' The car keys rattled as she raised her hand in a quick wave. 'Adieu, auf Wiedersehen and all that.'

Sam couldn't let her be so flippant. Stepping closer, he grabbed her hand. 'It's been great,' he said, not daring to offer anything more profound.

'It has,' Jenna agreed. And then, in a soft, almost breathless murmur. 'It's been amazing, Sam.'

And, of course, all he could think of then were the off-the-charts nights they'd shared.

'I look forward to hearing from you,' he said. 'In due course.'

Jenna nodded. 'In the meantime, all the best.'

Sam almost told her to drive safely, but he stopped himself before he sounded like some kind of nervous helicopter parent.

But he wished she wasn't wearing sunglasses. He wanted to see her lovely eyes one last time, wanted to read their mood, to try to divine their secrets. He wanted to kiss her too, but he knew that was wrong for all kinds of reasons, not least that Jenna wouldn't welcome such intimacy now at this point of departure.

So he simply gave a nod and stood with his hands sunk in his jeans pockets and watched as she got into her little car, backed out of the parking spot, then gave a brief toot of the horn and drove off.

IT WAS TWO nights later when Jenna rang. Sam was in the kitchen at Fenton, frying a couple of sausages for a late dinner when he saw her name light up his phone's screen. His spirits lit up as well, lifting like a popping champagne cork—a reaction so uncharacteristic he quite shocked himself.

What had happened to the Sam Twist who preferred women who were only in town temporarily? Now common sense voices inside his head were reminding him that his recent relationships had been getting shorter and shorter, less and less fun.

'Sam?' Jenna asked. 'Are you there?'

'Yeah, sure. Sorry, just wrestling with a frying pan.'

'Your dinner?'

'A-huh.'

'I'm eating mine now, too.' Jenna's voice was warm and friendly, as if she was smiling. 'You must dine as late as I do.'

He was tempted to ask her what she was eating and where. He would have liked to be able to picture her—in an apartment perhaps, or a café, or with a takeaway at her desk at the office.

He didn't ask, however, which was probably just as well, as Jenna wasted no further time on small talk. She didn't even enquire about Molly. She got straight to the point.

'So I've been talking to my colleagues, to the partners in my firm and they're on board.'

'That's a good start.'

'Yes, and they've agreed that we need to act quickly. I'm hoping to obtain a court order to enable you and Ted and the other farmers involved to at least gain access through the fence, so you can get your stock to the river.'

'Sounds great,' Sam said. 'Brilliant.'

'It's a first step at any rate.'

'It certainly is. Thanks, Jenna. I hope you can pull it off. As you know, Thorsborne are dead-serious.'

'Yes.'

'Word's out they've erected a demountable office on the site and have even installed two security officers to patrol the fence on bloody trail bikes.'

'Okay.' Jenna didn't sound too ruffled by this. 'They're moving fast, then.'

'Too right.' The sausages on the stove hissed and spat. Sam moved the pan away from the heat, so he could give her his full attention. 'They've also put up notices claiming that any straying stock found in the lease area will be impounded. And trespassers will be prosecuted.'

'Yes, well, that's par for the course.'

Sam was surprised she didn't sound more upset. 'It's downright provocation.'

'Not necessarily, Sam.'

'Of course it is. It's throwing petrol on the bloody fire.' He realised he'd raised his voice. In more measured tones, he added, 'Thorsborne's not just denying our access to the river, they're planning to steal our sheep and cattle if we dare to exercise our rights.'

'Always remembering that as things stand—without this court order—you don't currently have those rights. I'm afraid Thorsborne do have the law on their side.'

He couldn't help grinning. 'And do you know how dead sexy you sound when you talk like a lawyer?'

This was met by silence from the other end and Sam couldn't tell if he'd annoyed Jenna, or simply wrongfooted her.

'You're right, of course,' he said, wiping the grin and swiftly reverting to business. 'I've tried to explain to everyone here that Thorsborne have authority on their side, but the locals are so stirred up they don't want to listen. I've told them not to do anything foolish—there's a top city lawyer on the job. And old Ted's thrown in a good word for you. Reckons you'll give these bullies a legal punch in the nose.'

'Yes, well, everyone will need to be patient. I'm afraid the wheels of bureaucracy can be rather slow, but I'll certainly do my best.'

'And, as I said, we really appreciate this, Jenna. So thanks and good luck.'

It felt wrong though, to restrict a conversation with Jenna to this legal business, even though it was what they'd agreed on. Sam wanted to ask about *her*, how she was feeling, if she missed anything about Wirralong.

Jenna Matthews was different from any other girl he'd met. He'd been on the money when he'd said she bewitched him. She was like a fantasy woman—as lovely and clever as she was sensitive and caring—haunting his thoughts by day and his dreams by night.

'Goodnight, then, Sam,' she said now. 'I'll be in touch.'

So many things he wanted to tell her—silly romantic things like how much he missed her, or even how the lambs missed her—but he managed to restrain himself and kept his response to a minimum. 'Night, Jenna.'

THEY DIDN'T SPEAK again for almost a week. After another long, hot day on Fenton, Sam arrived back at the homestead and discovered he'd missed three calls from Jenna.

'Sorry,' he said when he rang her back. 'I've been check-ing boundaries. Must have dropped out of the network. How are you?'

'I'm fine, thanks.'

He would have liked more info about her than 'fine', but he knew better than to push. 'So, what's new?' he asked instead.

A beat passed before she answered. 'Do you want the good news or the bad news?'

Sam hadn't left the front verandah. Now he looked out at the paddocks where a pair of eagles was circling in the distance. Watching them, he grimaced. 'Better give me the bad news up front.'

Jenna gave a soft laugh. 'Okay, tough guy.'

'Yep,' he said, mentally bracing for the worst. 'Lay it on me.'

'Right.' Jenna paused, no doubt choosing her words care-fully, which only served to heighten his tension. 'I've done a more thorough check on Thorsborne and their mining lease and they've been very astute. They're a huge international company, of course, with offices in Toronto, London, Geneva and Paris—so clever heads are involved—and I'm afraid this is a much more difficult case than we expected.'

A band tightened around Sam's chest. 'In what way?'

Out on his paddock, one of the eagles dived earthwards, a sure sign that another of his ewes had died.

'Just over a year ago,' Jenna continued, 'the Authority to

Prospect was changed to an Agreement between the State Government and Thorsborne Mining. It actually involved an Act of Parliament.'

Sam frowned. 'I'm hearing you,' he said. 'But what exactly does that mean?'

'Basically, the Agreement has the full force of the law and only the Minister for Mines has the power to change anything. Which is highly unlikely, unless Thorsborne Mining also agree to any suggested variations.'

'In other words, the bastards can fence us off from the water and they have the government's support, so it's no use trying to get a court order against them?'

'I'm afraid so. The Act allows Thorsborne to establish their mine and all the relevant support facilities. And yes, in the Act's long list of required facilities there's a security fence listed.'

'Bastards.'

'I know. I'm sorry. I imagine the legislators would have been more than happy to tick off on any addition that involved workplace health and safety.'

'Of course they would. But they couldn't give a rat's arse about the farmers' mental health and safety.'

'I'm sure you're right.' Jenna sounded truly apologetic.

Remembering her tears, as she'd shared the terrible story about her father, Sam was gripped by a fierce urge to protect her, and yet here she was searching for ways to help him fight back.

'As far as the State is concerned,' Jenna went on. 'Thorsborne have met all their requirements, including notification of their intent to prospect and mine.'

'I suppose that explains the sign that showed up only recently, half-hidden in the scrub by the river?'

'I guess. Apparently there was also a public notice in the *Melbourne Age*.'

Swallowing a particularly unsavoury expletive, Sam turned his back on the scene of devastation out in his paddocks. Another of his sheep was being demolished by birds of prey and now his riparian rights had been signed away by smug city bureaucrats and a politician who was no doubt desperate to boast about economic development and job creation.

Bastards and bullshitters, the lot of them.

He felt suddenly very weary—and worried. He wasn't sure what Ted and the other graziers would do when they heard this news.

'So, you mentioned good news?' he asked. Not that he was hopeful.

'I did. We don't believe this is a totally lost cause, Sam.'

'How's that? You have something up your sleeve?'

'Yes.' There was the tiniest hint of excitement in Jenna's voice now. 'We slap Thorsborne Mining with a multimillion-dollar class action.'

Sam almost dropped his phone. 'You're joking.'

'Not at all. I've discussed it with my colleagues and

they're in favour. We can send a shock wave right through to the Thorsborne board room in Switzerland.'

'Wow.' Sam wasn't sure what to say. A class action seemed like a huge step. Way outside his experience or his expectations. 'You reckon you can pull it off?'

'It's a big call, but we have a solid case of aggrievement on behalf of the landholders whose livelihoods are threatened.'

He was leaning against a verandah railing now—stunned and more than a little elated. *Bloody hell, Jenna. How many surprises can one girl pull out of an almost empty hat?*

'You know you're amazing,' he said.

She laughed softly. 'I'm just doing my job.'

'No, you're not and you know it. You're going above and beyond.'

Jenna didn't respond to this. Sam supposed he was getting too personal and she might be worried he'd mention her father.

'So, what's the first step?' he asked.

'We'll need to hold a stakeholder meeting as soon as possible.'

'For all the graziers who've been affected?'

'Exactly. We need a recorded statement from every one of them—the amount of stock they carry, the size of their properties, their individual grievances, what they stand to lose—'

'Sounds fair enough. I can organise that.'

'I should warn you, though,' Jenna said next, 'there is a degree of risk.'

Sam inhaled sharply. 'In what way?'

'We can really twist Thorsborne's arm with the threat of a class action, but in these cases, there's usually one 'applicant' who takes the risk on behalf of all the others.'

'I see,' he said carefully.

'If it goes to court and the action fails, that person would, potentially, have to bear the costs.'

Thud. 'Which could be considerable.'

'Yes. Thorsborne's bound to go for the most expensive legal backup on offer.'

Sam thought of the dozen or more properties involved. These people were his neighbours. His community. Many of them, like his family, had lived here in the Wirralong district for generations.

Hard working, all of them, they were in this industry because they loved the land and the animals they raised here. It wasn't an easy life, having to deal with drought and floods and with markets that could rise or fall in a heartbeat, but they had learned to live with those challenges.

None of them should have to lose out to a mining giant.

It was important to take a stand.

'I'd be pre-'

Jenna cut him off. 'I don't want you jumping straight in and volunteering, Sam. I think it would be best if I explained the situation to everyone at the meeting. It's important to discuss this openly, so everyone's in the picture.'

'Okay, that's fair enough. So, I assume you'll be here in Wirralong for that meeting, too?'

He held his breath, waiting for her answer.

'Yes,' Jenna said. 'I'm taking this on. I'll be back.'

Chapter Twelve

A SHOCKING BUZZ hummed through Jenna as she prepared to return to Wirralong.

Unfortunately, the more she tried to ignore the buzz, the stronger it got, as if she'd been plugged into an electric current. And the buzz had nothing to do with the impending public meeting and class action. It was, regrettably, all about Sam.

Which was distressing. Jenna didn't want to admit, even to herself, that she missed Sam, that on the few occasions since leaving Wirralong when she'd spoken to him on the phone, she'd experienced a pain in her chest scarily close to what she imagined heartache might feel like.

She certainly didn't want to admit that being with Sam had been astonishingly easy, as well as exciting—almost as if they were a perfect match. She'd never had a relationship where she'd felt so 'on song.'

Seeing Sam again now, though, should not be a big deal. It couldn't be.

They'd had their fling. And, okay, maybe it had been the best fling weekend Jenna had ever experienced, and maybe her feelings for the man had become even more complicated when he'd been so nice about her weeping all over him. But those were not excuses for reliving every moment of her time at Wirralong on a dozen or more occasions in any given day.

Twice she'd been caught out at board meetings for not paying attention.

So. It was important now, before she left Melbourne, to accept finally, once and for all, that the fling with Sam Twist was over. Past tense. History.

Yes, she might be seeing him again soon, but she'd severely counselled herself against any thought of a repeat performance. Even to contemplate the possibility was dangerous when intimacy with the man was so addictive.

It would only make the next separation even harder. And Jenna certainly didn't want to fall into some kind of on-again, off-again affair with a guy who lived three hours' drive away. In the outback.

She and Sam were both defined by their work—as city lawyer and country grazier—and a future together was not and had never been an option for either of them. Jenna didn't do country and Sam wasn't about to sell Fenton and give up sheep farming. With sole responsibility for his property, he couldn't even get away for regular trips to Melbourne.

Jenna had this totally sorted in her head. She just wished she could get rid of the buzz. At times, when she allowed herself to think of Sam, her body was so busy humming, she could barely sit still at her desk.

'SO, I HEAR you and Sam really hit it off.'

Two days before the Wirralong public meeting, Cate rang, fresh from her Bali honeymoon.

'Welcome back to Oz,' Jenna quickly countered, hoping to head Cate in a totally different, Sam-free direction. 'And tell me about Bali. It sounds like the perfect choice for a honeymoon.'

'It was perfect for us,' Cate agreed. 'Just beautiful, Jen. The beaches were divine and the countryside was so lush and green, the total opposite of poor old drought-stricken Victoria right now.'

'Yeah, I can imagine.'

'The place where we stayed was off the main tourist drag and Craig and I just relaxed and—'

'Honeymooned?'

Cate laughed. 'Exactly.'

'I'm sure it was magical.'

'It was. Mind you, I don't think it would have mattered where we'd gone. I was just so over the moon happy to be with my guy.'

'That's wonderful,' Jenna said, before she remembered to edit the wistful note from her voice.

Perhaps Cate noticed, for in the next breath, she said,

'But back to the hot topic of you and Sam.'

Jenna didn't want to discuss her and Sam. But she knew Cate wouldn't let her get away with silence, so she said cautiously, 'Sam's a really nice guy.'

'Nice, my fat arse.' Cate snorted. 'You know very well he's all kinds of naughty.'

Jenna quickly switched her phone off speaker, relieved she was at home in her fifteenth-floor apartment and not at the office. 'Who've you been talking to, Cate?'

'Now let me see. I can think of at least four locals who might have mentioned that my bridesmaid and Craig's best man spent the weekend shacked up together.'

Jenna knew she shouldn't be surprised. Country towns were notorious hotbeds of gossip.

This evening, sitting at her kitchen bench with the remains of a takeaway Pad Thai, she looked out at her view through floor to ceiling windows to inner city Melbourne's tower blocks and busy streets. The night was illuminated by window-shaped squares of golden light and with snaking streams of headlights and taillights. The city. Her home. Her refuge.

Weird that she found herself thinking of Wirralong so often.

'It was just a fling with Sam,' she told Cate. 'Very pleasant while it lasted.'

'Well, yeah, I get that. And it's probably just as well to view it as temporary, Jenna.' Cate sounded quite serious now. 'When it comes to women, Sam's not so good at anything steady or long term.'

Knots tightened in Jenna's stomach—knots that made no sense. She should be reassured by Cate's comment. It backed up her own conclusions and requirements regarding Sam Twist.

'That's okay,' she said with false brightness. 'I don't do long-term either. And I certainly don't do country.'

'And yet you helped Sam to rescue orphaned lambs and got up at all sorts of hours to feed them?'

'Bloody hell, Cate. Who told you that?'

'The man himself.'

Traitor. 'It was two nights. And I could hardly lie around like Lady Muck and let Sam trudge out in the middle of the night to feed the sheep on his own.'

'Whatever. I think it was very sweet of you,' Cate said. 'And anyway, I was only teasing.'

'Mmm.' *And I fell for it hook, line and sinker.*

'I actually rang to thank you for getting involved in Dad's spot of bother with that damn fence.'

'Right.' Jenna let out her breath in a quick huff, surprised by how tense she'd been while Sam was the topic under discussion. Legal matters were so much safer. 'That's absolutely fine,' she said. 'I'm happy to lend a hand.'

'Everyone's gobsmacked about this class action. Dad can't stop talking about it.'

'It's good to have everyone on board,' said Jenna.

'And I believe you're coming back for a public meeting?'

'That's right. Two nights from now.'

'Will you stay with Sam?'

Whack! Jenna couldn't believe the way her heart took off at the mere mention of another night with Sam.

'Jenna, are you there?'

'Yes,' she managed, as she pressed a hand against her thudding chest. 'That is, yes, I'm here—but no, I won't be staying at Fenton. I'll be at the pub again.'

'Oh.' It was hard to tell what Cate thought of this news. 'Okay. We'll have to catch up.'

'Sure. Lovely.'

'Actually, Craig and I would love to have you and Sam out to our place. Just something simple—probably a barbecue.'

'Right,' Jenna said cautiously.

'Our place is pretty modest, mind you.'

Jenna knew Craig had converted the old shearers' quarters on Longholme into somewhere for him and Cate to live. It meant they had their own little place on the property, some distance away from his parents.

Jenna was keen to see Cate's new home, but given her reaction to the possibility of another 'fling', she wasn't totally okay about attending another social event with Sam. From now until this case was settled one way or the other, keeping things on a strictly business footing was the only sensible option.

Then again, Sam was Craig's best mate, so of course he'd be invited, too.

'I'd love to come,' Jenna said. 'I'm really looking forward to seeing your new home. Thanks.'

'Great. We can go back out there after the meeting. It'll be nice to chill after all the business.'

'It will,' Jenna agreed. 'By the way, did Sam mention how the lambs are doing?'

Cate burst into peals of laughter.

Chapter Thirteen

S AM MET JENNA at the door of Wirralong's School of Arts, where the meeting was to be held. He was dressed in pale chinos and a blue-and-white striped shirt with button down pockets and sleeves rolled back to his elbows. This was pretty much a uniform for men of the land, a look Jenna had never found sexy. Until now.

Unfortunately for her, the extra breadth of Sam's shoulders, the leanness of his hips and the cheeky twinkle in his grey eyes could make sackcloth and ashes look sexy.

Damn him. Being distracted by Sam Twist before the meeting had even started was certainly not part of her plan.

'Great to see you again.' Sam stepped forward to kiss her cheek, an act which, of necessity, involved contact with his smoothly shaved jaw and a waft of spicy aftershave.

In a flash, the buzzing issues Jenna had been battling since leaving Wirralong went into overdrive. Dragging in a deep breath, she desperately tried to blank out memories of the smooth planes and muscles to be found beneath Sam's fine cotton shirt.

'You're looking very lawyerly,' he said, letting his gaze

linger, as he very deliberately checked her out.

She had been aiming for a businesslike image, of course, and she'd teamed a demure, plain grey, pintucked blouse with a black, knee-length pencil skirt. But Sam's sparkling-eyed grin couldn't have been cheekier if she'd been wearing a kinky nurse's outfit that barely covered her bum.

She chose to ignore his comment and shifted her attention to the people who filled the rows of seats inside the hall. 'Looks like a good roll up,' she said.

Sam nodded. 'All your stakeholders are here already, plus a fair support crowd.'

Jenna could see Ted Jeffries sitting at the front with Cate and Craig beside him. Cate turned just then and, on seeing Jenna, immediately left her seat to hurry to the back of the hall.

'Hey, beautiful,' she cried, throwing her arms around Jenna for a crushing hug. 'It's so good to see you.'

'You, too,' Jenna told her. 'You look wonderful. Just glowing. Married life clearly suits you.'

Cate grinned. 'I reckon it does. That and getting out of the city.'

Jenna's smile at this last comment was muted in response. She'd been somewhat surprised today, while heading north from Melbourne, to find herself looking forward to the eucalypt-dotted paddocks of the Wirralong district with the magnificent Grampian Mountains as their backdrop.

'Anyway,' Cate said. 'All the best for this afternoon. I

think you'll find everyone's keen to cooperate any way they can.'

Jenna nodded. She couldn't help feeling a little tense now with so many people depending on her.

'And we're really looking forward to seeing you two later for the barbecue,' Cate added, flashing an extra bright smile that included Sam.

'Too right,' agreed Sam.

Again Jenna nodded, but she didn't allow herself to meet Sam's gaze as Cate returned to her seat.

NERVOUS WAS THE polite word for how Sam felt as the stakeholder meeting began. He couldn't tell if Jenna was nervous, too. He knew it was her job to handle such cases, but he still couldn't help but remember her original plan had been to use one of her colleagues and he felt guilty about dragging her into this mess.

She looked calm, though, and all kinds of beautiful, as she faced the hall filled with Wirralong locals, many of whom were fired up and looking for a fight.

Jenna thanked everyone for coming and lightened the mood by referring to their situation as 'Fencegate.' Then she explained that she would need a register of all the people whose properties were directly affected by said fence.

She already had a good idea of the numbers, apparently,

but she would collect their names and contact details at this meeting. Over the next couple of days, an assistant from her firm would be in touch to record each story and grievance.

Jenna went on to explain her firm's plans for the class action, hitting Thorsborne Mining for around twelve million dollars—a million for each of the properties affected—with the best outcome being an out-of-court settlement and, hopefully, mediation.

Of course there were questions, including how Jenna had arrived at the figure of twelve million.

'It's an ambient claim,' she explained. 'Even though most of you have dams and bores, the lack of access to the river means potential serious stock loss, as well as a significant downturn in the value of your land. It would be hard to sell a riverfront property with no access to that water.'

Ted Jeffries stood up. 'I wish you all the best with this, lass, but to be honest, I'm not looking for money from these people. I just want my rights to the water back. That said, I really like the idea of taking the fight to them.'

Unsurprisingly, this was greeted by cheers and applause. It seemed everyone was keen to press ahead.

Jenna was smiling, too, but then her expression grew serious as she held up her hand for quiet. 'It's great to have you all on board,' she said. 'But I'm afraid this action isn't without risks.'

Sam sat straighter, knowing what was coming next.

'A class action requires an applicant to launch it on behalf of all the aggrieved parties,' Jenna said.

'You mean one of us?' called a voice.

'Yes,' said Jenna. 'But I should—'

Ted Jeffries's hand shot up. 'I'm willing.'

Jenna held him at bay with a cautioning gesture. 'Thanks, Ted, that's very generous, but there are a few things all of you need to understand before anyone volunteers.'

Sam sensed a ripple of tension through the crowd, wind on the surface of a pond.

'I have to be honest and warn you,' Jenna continued. 'Whoever takes on the role of class applicant runs a serious financial risk. If we don't get a settlement and our class action case goes all the way to court—and is then lost—the applicant is personally liable.'

The room was pin-drop silent now, as if everyone had taken a collective gulp.

'A big mining company like Thorsborne would almost certainly hire the most expensive legal people in the country,' she went on. 'The costs could really mount up.'

Sam realised his teeth were tightly clenched—and he'd been forewarned. He could imagine the tension rioting through the audience now. Was this gamble worth the risk of losing a family property?

Barry Fraser, a large, red-faced cattleman who was new to the district, was on his feet now. 'Speaking of legal costs,' he bellowed to Jenna from his position near the back. 'What will you get out of this?'

Several heads were nodding, and there was a flurry of murmured whispers.

Jenna gave them a dignified smile. 'I sincerely hope this will be settled out of court and, if it is, I won't receive anything. My partners have agreed that I can take this case pro bono.'

Another murmur of surprise.

'So let me get this straight,' Barry Fraser challenged, hands firmly on hips. 'If we go to court and we lose, some-one here could end up in a hell of a lot of trouble. And if we win, we'd end up with a share of a million dollars for each property, and still no access to the river?'

Sam jumped to his feet before Jenna could reply. He could see this going pear-shaped, if someone didn't back her.

She sent him a cautious smile, but her expression was full of question marks.

Sam turned to the crowd. 'We have to trust that Jenna will get this settled out of court,' he said and there were nods of approval, as well as a few frowns and scowls. 'She's told us that mediation is her primary aim. But we need a class action as a backup, as part of our legal weaponry.'

Pausing, he caught Jenna's eye again. 'Have I got that right?'

She nodded. 'The risk for the applicant comes if the class action fails. But no-one else will have any risk if the case goes against Thorsborne, and everyone benefits if we have a victory.'

Her expression was very serious now, almost as if she might be able to guess what Sam was about to do next.

He wondered if she was thinking of her father, remembering the man who'd lost his own personal battle with the drought, leaving a terrible legacy of anguish and heartbreak.

In the next flickering second Sam thought of Fenton, his family's beloved home and source of livelihood. Now, for possibly the first time in four generations, battle lines had been drawn. But he couldn't back down.

Not caring that an entire hall full of locals were watching, he offered Jenna his warmest, most confident smile.

'If someone has to stand up,' he said next. 'I'm prepared to do it.'

The hall exploded with a loud burst of applause.

'ARE YOU SURE you're quite comfortable with this decision, Sam?'

They were in his SUV, preparing to drive to Longholme, but Jenna didn't want to set off till she and Sam had debriefed.

'I'm fine with it.' He sounded quite certain and she sensed a squaring of his jaw, as if he was preparing for some kind of battle. 'I started this fight. I cut the bloody fence, so it's only right that I should cop responsibility.'

Jenna nodded. 'Okay. I know everyone's very grateful.'

'Not that I want to lose Fenton, of course,' he added.

'No,' Jenna agreed. 'We certainly don't want that. I'm doing my best to get a third-party litigation fund company on board.'

Sam's eyes widened. 'Excuse me? A what?'

'A litigation fund company. They're specially set up to fund class actions. They enter into an agreement to pay the legal costs and accept liability if the class action is unsuccessful. But if it's successful, they get their money back, plus a share of the settlement.'

'Wow. So they're like an insurance company?'

'More or less. I didn't mention it at the meeting, because I'm still hunting for the perfect group to take this on. They can take a little persuading, but it's early days and I'm confident.'

Sam smiled. 'And that's good enough for me.'

He looked like he wanted to kiss her then, but a crowd from the hall was lingering on the footpath, all within eyesight. So Jenna had to be content with another of his cheeky smiles.

Chapter Fourteen

CRACKLING LOGS GLOWED in a firepit and the black night sky glittered with diamond-bright stars. Jenna, now changed into jeans and a casual denim shirt, was ensconced in a canvas squatter's chair, wine glass in hand, and cocooned by an unexpected sense of contentment.

For the first time since her childhood, she was outdoors in the bush at night and not nearly as freaked as she'd feared she might be. In fact, everything about this evening's experience had been exceptionally pleasant, even calming.

She'd actually been scared about the meeting in Wirralong, about facing a hall full of troubled, drought-plagued farmers. Every night for a week she'd had nightmares about her dad and the dreaded shadow she'd witnessed on the machinery shed floor.

But none of the Wirralong locals had seemed particularly distressed and the meeting had concluded on a gratifyingly optimistic note. Afterwards, Sam had been relaxed and as charming as ever as he'd driven out to Longholme. And, for her part, Jenna was satisfied that they had a solid case and that she had all bases covered.

So she might have been relaxed, too, if she hadn't been bothered by the whole zapping and buzzing thing, times one hundred.

At least their arrival at Longholme had been a helpful distraction. It had been fun inspecting Craig's fabulous conversion of the shearing shed. He'd used an interesting mix of recycled windows and doors and a fab combo of timber, corrugated iron and concrete to create a truly comfy home with a trendy-but-rustic vibe.

'It's absolutely gorgeous, Cate.' Jenna was seriously impressed and happy for her friend. 'This is like a home you'd see in a magazine.'

'I know.' Cate's grin was wide. 'I'm so proud of Craig. Mind you,' she added with a wink, 'I've been his project manager.'

'Ah,' Jenna responded with an answering grin. 'So that explains the artistic touches.'

'Oh, for sure. My input, plus the help of a gazillion Pinterest pics.'

While the chops sizzled on the barbecue, the foursome sat around the fire pit, enjoying the carefully selected wines and cheeses that Jenna had brought from her favourite deli at the Melbourne markets.

'What? No mushroom chips or pickled baby octopus?' Cate teased.

Jenna smiled. She'd been tempted to bring a selection of the trendier deli items, but she'd imagined Craig and Sam scoffing at such urban wankery. Now, though, having seen Craig's craftsmanship in their new home and the delicious meal he and Cate had prepared, including a scrumptious gourmet salad of broccoli with cranberries and toasted slivered almonds, Jenna realised she'd once again been the victim of her own snobbish assumptions.

And now, as a cool night breeze drifted over the land and a boat-shaped, golden moon sailed across the beautiful starry sky, the security screen that, for two decades, had stood between Jenna's safe city life and the vast Australian outback was as full of holes as a colander.

And that was only a minor problem compared with her crazy, over-the-top reaction to Sam's proximity, which continued relentlessly throughout the evening.

Conversation around the fire was relaxed and light, however, steering away from the topics of drought and problem fences. They talked about Bali and other travel destinations and shared jokes and funny stories.

Craig and Sam were both good storytellers and Jenna actually managed to tell a lawyer joke that everyone laughed at. There'd been plenty of laughter all evening, in fact, and she'd loved every moment—every glimpse of Sam's profile in the flickering firelight, every shared smile. She'd loved the timbre of his voice as he'd told his stories, the brush of his hand as he refilled her glass, reminding her of the private memories they shared.

Tipping her head back, she looked again at the sky, deliberately forcing her thoughts elsewhere. Everything was so bright and clear here, away from the city lights. The half-moon looked exactly like a dinghy adrift in a sea of stars. 'Don't they say the moon needs to tip on its side before it can rain?' she said.

Sam frowned. 'Who says that?'

Jenna shrugged. 'I don't know. Old wives, I suppose. If the moon tips, the rain will spill out.'

'Not going to happen tonight,' said Cate, glumly staring overhead.

'No.' Jenna continued to watch the awesome sky. 'It's amazing though, isn't it, to think that the Aborigines were looking at this same moon thousands of years before Captain Cook arrived. And the Aztecs and the Incas. The Mongols, the Vikings.'

'You're in an interesting mood,' Cate observed, sending her a hard-to-read smile.

Jenna laughed softly. She couldn't exactly confess that she was carrying on about the moon in a desperate attempt to distract herself from obsessing about Sam.

The man was a hazard. No question. He'd not only seduced her body. He'd touched her emotions and had won her respect. And it didn't seem to matter that she'd received many warnings about his unsuitability as a romantic interest, delivered by both her own common sense and by Cate.

She couldn't stop obsessing about how much she wanted him.

Just one more time …

When she and Sam finally said goodnight and climbed back into his SUV, she was a ticking time bomb about to detonate.

'THAT WAS A lovely night, wasn't it?' she said, as they whizzed back down the highway, headlights spearing ahead through the darkness.

'Yeah,' Sam agreed. 'Those two are a great pair. Reckon they did the right thing getting hitched.'

'Cate's slipped straight back into country life like she's never left.'

'I guess.' In the dark of the vehicle's cabin, Jenna sensed Sam turn to her. 'Does that surprise you?'

'A bit. Seven months ago, I would have sworn Cate was a totally committed city girl.'

'The city and the country don't have to be mutually exclusive, do they? It's not as if you can only enjoy one or the other?'

Jenna sighed. 'That's the way it's always seemed to me.'

A beat or two passed before Sam responded. 'Maybe Cate's an exception then.'

'Or perhaps I am,' Jenna said softly.

There was another longish pause before Sam spoke again. 'There's no doubting you're exceptional, Jenna.'

She heard the unexpected tenderness in his voice and she wasn't sure what to say. She almost begged him to stop the car, there and then, but if he did, she knew she would almost certainly hurl herself into his arms.

Yikes. She was supposed to be sensible about this. She'd promised herself she would be extremely sensible, but now that she was quite alone with Sam, her willpower was crumpling like paper thrown on fire.

Crossing her arms tightly over her chest, Jenna stared resolutely at the road ahead. And then she crossed her legs for good measure.

This course of action wasn't much help, though. Her lustier self was still busily planning ahead, thinking of the intersection where Sam could turn right to Fenton, or continue straight ahead into town.

She imagined him turning right, driving back to his place, because he couldn't pass up this opportunity and he knew, intuitively, how badly she wanted him. She was quite sure the need was mutual. The messages had been coming off him all night, like radio waves.

So she could picture how it would happen—pulling up outside Sam's homestead, getting out of the vehicle to find him already there, ready and waiting, his arms wide. They would fall into a kiss straight away—hungry nibble kisses, perhaps, excited and breathless—and they would stumble a little as they kept trying to kiss while they made their way up the steps and into the house. Sam would undo her shirt, which had buttons all the way down the front. He'd do this feverishly, or perhaps he'd take his time and stop to kiss her neck, the dip of her collarbone, the soft swell of her breasts.

Fast or slow, either way would suit Jenna. She wasn't fussy. And they would leave a trail of clothes behind them, across the living room floor, down the hallway, as they made their way to his bedroom. And then the fun would really begin ...

Ohhhh.

'Are you okay?'

Jenna gulped. Had she really moaned out loud?

'Yes, I'm fine,' she said, and she tried to be super, *super* sensible for the next kilometre, until Sam slowed down to give way to a huge cattle train that was approaching the intersection ahead.

This was the crucial moment. As soon as the road was clear, Sam would turn right, heading for Fenton. Jenna smiled to herself, almost purring and squirming with expectant pleasure.

The cattle train roared through the intersection, Sam accelerated again and she held her breath, waiting for him to indicate a right-hand turn.

He continued straight ahead.

'Oh.'

In the faint light thrown by the dashboard, she saw Sam's frown. 'Are you sure you're okay?'

No, Jenna wanted to tell him. *I'm crumbling with disap-*

pointment, falling into a thousand desolate pieces.

But how could she tell him this? What kind of demented woman told a man that he should have been able to guess how badly she wanted to have wild, all-night sex with him? Even though she'd made it excruciatingly clear that he should keep his distance?

Bloody hell.

She'd made a huge song and dance about only wanting that one fling on the wedding weekend, and she'd voiced this not only to Sam, but to Cate as well. Chances were, Cate had reinforced this message with Sam, warning him—or possibly reassuring him—that Jenna would not want or expect a deeper entanglement.

In other words, she'd got exactly what she'd asked for. It made no sense that she was totally devastated.

'I'm fine,' she told Sam again now, suppressing her deep disappointment as she answered his question. 'Just tired, I guess.'

In fact, as her excited anticipation gave way to dashed hopes, she did feel rather tired now. This day had, in reality, been quite a long one, beginning with an early morning pile of paperwork at the city office, followed by the three-hour drive out to Wirralong and the subsequent meeting, before continuing on to the barbecue.

Thinking about all of this, Jenna yawned.

'I hope we haven't kept you up too late,' Sam said.

'No.' In the darkness, she allowed herself a rueful smile.

'Will you have to feed the lambs when you get home?'

'Yeah,' he said. 'They'll be on the bottle for a few weeks yet. I actually have four orphans now.'

You need me to help you. The words were on the tip of her tongue. She imagined saying them out loud, pictured Sam slamming on the brakes and then turning around and driving back to his homestead. She could even picture the two of them laughing together as they sped back down the highway, jubilant that they hadn't missed out on the perfect opportunity for another night together ...

'You must be busy,' she said instead and, to her utter dismay, the closer she got to Wirralong, the louder the voice of her common sense sounded.

At least, when Sam pulled up outside the Wirralong Hotel, the reception desk, which was quite visible from the street, was empty. Jenna sat very still for a moment or two, willing her knees to stop shaking before she climbed out.

'I'll be in touch, as soon as I have any news, especially if I have a date for the class action,' she said.

'That'd be great. Thanks. And good luck with getting that litigation fund whatsername.'

'Thanks. I'll let you know about that, too.'

Sam nodded. 'Thanks for everything, Jenna.'

'My pleasure,' she said softly.

He reached for her hand, linking his fingers with hers and sending fine tremors all over her skin. Every cell in her longed to curl closer. She wanted to tell him she'd missed him, that she hadn't stopped thinking about him. And perhaps, if he'd made the slightest move towards her, she might have done exactly that. But apart from holding her hand, Sam remained perfectly still.

Good, she told herself sadly. *This is how it should be.*

He stroked her hand with his thumb. 'Take care, won't you?'

TAKE CARE?

What kind of lame-brained farewell was that? Sam couldn't believe he was sitting here, like a gormless teenager who had no idea what to do with a beautiful girl.

So many times tonight he'd wanted to drop not-so-subtle suggestions to Jenna. Driving her home, he'd very nearly veered off in the direction of Fenton, while mentally composing lines of perfect seduction.

By now, they could have been in bed and naked.

Yeah, right. Sam wrenched his thoughts back to reality and the fact that he was a novice when it came to this whole lawyer–client scenario.

On the weekend that he'd met Jenna, she'd been a bridesmaid and he'd been best man at their mutual friends' wedding and taking her home had been straightforward—not to mention spectacular. Now, damn it, he'd had a writ served against him and he'd put his hand up to represent his neighbours in this class action, and the girl sitting beside him had morphed from dream lover into city-based courtroom saviour.

The fact that Sam wanted her more than any woman he'd ever known was a complication he'd never anticipated. Even more confusing—he'd discovered that his avoidance of a long-term romance no longer made sense. Seemed the sprinter had set his sights on a marathon with the one girl who wouldn't be interested. An impossible situation all round.

And now, with Jenna's hand so small in his, he was excruciatingly aware of the warmth of her palm, of the innocent but reassuring intimacy of their interlocked fingers.

Light from the hotel's foyer spilled through plate glass windows across the footpath to reach the car's interior, showing him her profile. Her neat nose and determined chin, her soft, ever-so-kissable mouth.

He drew a deep breath, let it out slowly. Then, lifting her hand to his lips, he kissed it gently. 'Night, Jenna.'

'Goodnight.' Her voice was small and tight as he released her hand, and without looking his way again, she undid her seat belt, opened the passenger door and hopped out. 'I'll call you,' she said again as she slammed the door shut and she sounded angry.

Sam could only stare as she marched off into the hotel. What the hell was that about?

Chapter Fifteen

A S SLEEPLESS NIGHTS went, this was about the worst Jenna had experienced and she knew it was her own fault. Her farewell with Sam had been so unsatisfactory. She'd more or less flounced away from him in a huff of frustration, like a petulant, self-obsessed teenager.

She'd never been quite so annoyed with herself, had never before let a man get under her skin the way Sam had. Had never spent such a tortured night, tossing and turning, reliving each tantalising memory, as well as the more recent moments that she should have handled so much better.

Damn it—if she'd simply let Sam know that she was hot for one more night with him, he would have headed straight back to his place and they would have had fantastic sex. Afterwards, they would have said goodbye like adults and she wouldn't be left with all the crazy what-ifs that had kept her awake all night.

Now, as Jenna showered and dressed in preparation for her return to the city, she felt drained and exhausted and as flattened as roadkill. When her phone rang, she almost ignored it, but at the last moment she glanced at the screen.

The caller was Sam.

She also found two missed calls from him that must have come while she was in the shower. Her ridiculous heart flipped as she pressed the button to answer his call, flipped again when she heard his voice.

'Jenna.'

'Hi, Sam.' At least she managed to sound fairly casual.

'Are you still in town?'

'Ah—' Jenna's thoughts were spinning as she tried to guess where this was headed.

'That isn't a trick question,' Sam added.

She heard the smile in his voice and could picture the exact curve of his lips, the creases around his sparkling eyes.

'I need your advice,' he said. 'Can you spare a moment?'

'Of course.' Advice she could manage. She breathed more easily now. 'How can I help?'

'I have a news team on my doorstep.'

Wow. Jenna supposed she should have anticipated this. 'Television news?'

'Yeah. The whole box and dice—that journalist, Polly Horton, her cameraman and some kind of sound guy.'

Jenna knew Polly Horton, the court reporter from Channel Nine. Polly and her crew would be all over Sam with his outdoorsy good looks and cheeky grin. Oh, yeah. They'd be dead keen to film him in his battered jeans and faded work shirt, all suntanned and rugged and sexy. 'I suppose they want to film the fence?' she said.

'Yeah, the fence, my property, whatever I can show them, but I've been holding them off till I got your okay. I thought—if you're still around, you might want to handle this.'

'Yes.' It certainly made sense for her to be there as back-up. 'Yes, all right. I'll be there as soon as I can.' Jenna hadn't had breakfast and she was starving after her restless night, but food would have to wait. She was heading back to Fenton. 'I guess they'll be getting fidgety,' she said.

'Yep. I'm about to give them a cup of tea and toast. Right now they're feeding the lambs and—'

'The lambs?' Jenna cried. 'Actually feeding them?' Sam had let Polly Horton feed *her* lambs?

'Well, yeah. It's keeping them entertained,' he said. 'But they're keen to get on with the filming.'

'Of course.' Jenna was annoyed by her overreaction. *Yet again*. 'Let them take footage of your property and the river, or whatever. You should be fine if you just stick to explaining your circumstances. Just leave anything to do with the courts or law to me.'

'Will do. Sorry if this delays you, but thanks, Jenna.'

Sam's voice was warm, his words sincere. They made her chest ache.

'See you soon,' she said.

GOING BACK TO Fenton should not have been a sentimental journey, but Jenna found herself viewing each bend in the road, each bridge and gatepost with ridiculously warm nostalgia. When she turned in at Sam's front gate and saw the track leading across the familiar paddocks dotted with sheep and gumtrees, she had the most disturbing sense of coming home.

How crazy was that? Just as well there'd be a TV crew here to keep her from doing or saying anything foolish.

Even so, her heart gave a painful little clunk when Sam emerged from the homestead and came down the steps to greet her. The clunk became a rapid drumbeat when he leaned in and kissed her cheek. 'Great to see you again,' he said and then he grinned as he looked her over. She was in her pencil skirt and high heels with a silky grey-and-green-striped top. 'Ready for work, I see.'

'Of course.' She looked around for the news crew's vehicle. 'Where are they?'

Sam cocked his head towards the river. 'Already down there, setting up.'

'Right.' Somehow Jenna had expected to meet them in the homestead. It wouldn't be easy to negotiate a riverbank in a tight skirt and high heels.

'We'll go down there in my ute,' Sam said.

'Okay.'

He looked again at her clothes and his mouth tilted in a crooked smile. 'The ute might not be the cleanest. Do you want one of my shirts or something to cover up?'

Jenna knew she should probably change and she did have more suitable clothes in her car, but she also knew she should be in and out of this place as quickly as she could manage. Any delays around Sam were dangerous. 'No, I'll be fine,' she said.

Except that she wasn't fine. Climbing back into his ute with its lingering scent of hay and dust reminded her of the Sunday afternoon they'd spent traversing his paddocks and distributing stock feed ... and the evening that had followed.

Once again, she was fighting the strangest sense of belonging, of being at home.

The sooner she got back to Melbourne, the better.

POLLY HORTON AND her team were set up and waiting when Sam and Jenna arrived. The river bank was relatively low at this point and the wide bed was mostly sand with the only available water blocked off by the newly repaired fence.

Polly, dressed appropriately for the bush in jeans and a pink linen shirt, was clearly surprised when she saw Jenna.

'Jenna Matthews?' she exclaimed, her carefully made-up eyes agog. 'What are you doing here?'

'I'm looking after this case.'

'But you never—' Polly stopped in mid-sentence as she let her gaze travel over Jenna in her businesslike city garb and then over Sam. Eventually, a slow knowing smile dawned. 'Right,' she said. 'I see.' And her tone implied that she saw a whole lot more than a troubled grazier and his lawyer.

Jenna was glad she was wearing sunglasses. Just the same, she took extra care to keep her face poker straight.

Of course Polly wanted Sam and Jenna together for the footage. Jenna did try to suggest that Sam on his own would be fine, but both Polly and her cameraman insisted that the story needed the two of them.

Sam was his natural, charming self as he explained about the generations of his family that had lived on this property, about the effects of the drought and the writ served against him for cutting the fence that had denied his cattle access to water. When it was Jenna's turn, she also kept her story straight down the line.

This was about farmers' basic rights. Mr Twist and the other property owners along this river were dealing with tough drought conditions and they couldn't rely on wells and farm dams to cover their requirements. Their obvious need for a supplementary water supply had been overridden by new legislation regarding Thorsborne's mining lease.

She wouldn't be drawn into speculating whether the legislation had been drafted intentionally or in error.

'We believe we have a strong case,' she said. 'Thorsborne aren't budging and we're prepared to take this to the highest levels.'

Polly looked pleased as she thanked them. 'Just one final

question,' she said as Jenna backed away from the camera with a marked sense of relief.

Jenna tried not to scowl. 'Yes?'

'Jenna Matthews, you're well known in city circles as a successful corporate lawyer and this story is very different from your usual focus. Can you tell us why you've taken a special interest in this case?'

Jenna swallowed. The camera was trained directly on her, probably in close up, and she knew she'd paused a tell-tale shade too long. She didn't dare glance towards Sam. 'I look after a wide range of cases,' she said. 'And people in rural areas are as entitled to justice as people in the city.'

'That's true,' Polly responded, obviously keen to push her point. 'But you don't usually—'

'Thank you. I have no more to say on this,' Jenna said, interrupting her and again turning her back on the camera.

'Sam,' Polly tried again. 'You must be very pleased to have such a high-profile lawyer supporting your case.'

Sam's smoky gaze met Jenna's and try as she might to remain stony faced, she felt sparks shooting in all directions. Damn. She hated to think what the camera had caught.

Shaking her head to silence him, she said, 'I think we're finished here and I really must be on my way.'

Luckily, Sam took his cue. 'Thanks, everyone,' he said with an air of finality. 'I really appreciate your interest in this, but you heard Ms Matthews. She needs to get back to Melbourne.'

Jenna's exit would have been much more dignified if her spindly heels hadn't sunk so deeply into the sandy earth. There was a dangerous moment when she stumbled and might have fallen without Sam's strong hand at her elbow.

She didn't dare to look back and she hoped to high heaven that the camera was no longer filming.

Once safely in the ute, she let out a huff of relief.

Sam didn't speak as he gunned the motor. His expression was serious and she had no idea what he was thinking. Which was fine. His thoughts were his own business, not hers.

Except that her curiosity was killing her.

His silence continued, however, as they drove over the bumpy track back to the homestead, where her little car was parked out the front, looking like a shiny, blue exotic beetle, as out of place in this rural landscape as she was.

She felt inexplicably downbeat as Sam slowed the ute to a halt. 'Would you like a cuppa before you head off?' he asked, remaining quite still in his seat.

His jeans-covered thighs were so close. So intensely masculine. And his hands were still on the steering wheel, strong and suntanned. His shirt sleeves were rolled back leaving exposed forearms, also strong and tanned, covered in light golden hairs.

He was inviting her inside.

Jenna pictured herself in his sunny, comfy kitchen, with Gerry curled in a corner, while she enjoyed a coffee and perhaps a microwaved scone from the stash in the freezer. She imagined checking out the lambs—four of them now. Imagined Sam persuading her to stay on—

So tempting, for all the wrong reasons.

Just as well there was a TV camera crew following them, or she might have leaped into his lap and behaved very badly.

'I really must get going,' she said.

Sam nodded grimly. 'Of course.'

They both climbed out of the ute.

'Thanks again,' Sam said.

'I'm not sure you really needed me. You handled that well.'

His throat worked. 'It was good to have your backup.'

Jenna nodded. 'I'll be in touch.'

'Yeah, you do that.' He said this in that slow easy way of his that curled around her, tying her in knots.

She might have kissed him then if she hadn't seen the cloud of dust signalling the journalists' return.

'Bye, Sam.'

As she drove away, she could see him in the rear-view mirror, standing in front of his homestead, his hands resting lightly on his hips. Tall, broad shouldered. And solitary.

The vision blurred as her eyes filled with tears.

Chapter Sixteen

I T WAS STILL dark when Sam left home on the morning of the class action, dressed in a business suit. Apart from the penguin suit he'd worn for Craig's wedding, he couldn't remember the last time he'd been in a coat and tie—at his father's funeral, perhaps. Hettie Green, his cleaning woman, had aired and pressed the charcoal-grey suit and Sam had teamed it with a white shirt and conservative grey-and-silver tie.

He grimaced at his almost unrecognisable reflection in the mirror. Perhaps Jenna was right. City and country didn't mix.

Shrugging this uncomfortable thought aside, he left Gerry in her basket on the verandah, guarding the front door, and headed out of the house. He hadn't bothered with breakfast, but bought a takeaway coffee when he filled his vehicle with petrol on the outskirts of town. By this time, a faint rosy glow shimmered on the horizon.

First light was normally Sam's favourite time of day. He enjoyed a sense of optimism while watching the night sky fade and the landscape emerge in the gentle early light. This morning, however, even the dawn couldn't cheer him.

For weeks he'd been in a grim mood that wouldn't lift. Everyone in the district was on tenterhooks about the class action, of course, and the continuing drought hadn't helped. Nor had the fact that in all that time, the only contact he'd received from Jenna had come via a few, curt and business-like text messages.

The first text brought the good news that Jenna had acquired a third-party litigation fund company for their case. Which should have been a huge relief. It meant Sam's chances of losing Fenton were now minimal. A week or so later, Jenna had texted him again with the scheduled date, time and Melbourne address for the class action.

Naturally, after each text, Sam had tried to call her back, but he could only reach her voice mail.

In frustration, he'd written: *Do we need to plan a strategy for this meeting?*

Not really, she'd replied. *Play it cool and just follow my lead and you'll be fine.*

Sam, used to fighting his own battles, had no choice but to fall in line. And the low mood had persisted. He didn't want to admit it was caused by Jenna's obvious decision to cut all personal ties with him as she reverted to city-based corporate lawyer.

Their fling weekend, the night of the barbecue at Long-holme, even the lambs had all been relegated to the past. Done and dusted.

To Sam's annoyance, he wasn't nearly as okay about this as he should have been. Just the same, he wasn't prepared to persist when the message from Jenna was so damn clear.

He had no choice but to cop it sweet. If the case went well today, he and Jenna Matthews would have no further need to communicate and he could close the book on a short but unforgettable chapter in his life.

Perhaps, when this was over, the memories that plagued him would fade.

THE MEETING WITH Thorsborne executives was to be held on the twenty-third floor of an inner-city office block. Sam arrived promptly at ten-thirty, and Jenna was already there, waiting for him, blonde hair immaculately in place and wearing a knock-em-dead, black-and-white dress. Sam thought she was a little thinner perhaps—although she hadn't needed to lose weight—and her demeanour was certainly more cautious than ever.

His smile was as careful as hers when she shook his hand. Shook his hand, mind you. Not even a peck on the cheek.

'Good to see you,' he said.

'You, too, Sam. How was the trip?'

'Fine.'

Her formal politeness irked him and he looked around, expecting to see at least one of her colleagues in tow, but no one was visible. 'You're on your own?'

'I am, yes. We don't want to confront these people with a war party.' Jenna nodded to the briefcase at her feet—impressive leather, but not exactly bulging with a promising wad of legal paperwork. 'I have everything I need. We'll be fine with just the two of us.' She let her bewitching green gaze travel over his suit.

'Is my tie straight?' he challenged.

'Almost.' The colour in her cheeks deepened to a becoming pink as she stepped forward and made a slight adjustment. He caught a whiff of her perfume, like a flower-filled meadow. 'There,' she said. 'You look—' Her lovely mouth twisted in a complicated smile that just might have carried a hint of sadness. 'You look perfect.'

It took all Sam's strength to keep his distance from her then, but his restraint was probably well advised. At that very moment, a journalist burst through sliding glass doors to accost them, phone in hand.

Sam drew a sharp breath as the guy introduced himself. He supposed he should have expected another onslaught from the media. After the Channel Nine story there'd been more reporters in Wirralong. Even *The Age* had run a story in its business and legal section about the big multi-national mining company being challenged by northeast Victorian farmers who claimed they'd lost their riparian rights.

In the story, Jenna had been referred to yet again as a 'well-regarded, high-profile corporate lawyer.' Nevertheless, there'd been speculation that this could be a David and Goliath battle, if it went to court.

'I'll address all of the media inside,' Jenna told the fellow as she picked up her briefcase and shot Sam a quick, careful glance. 'Okay,' she said. 'Let's go.'

The glass doors slid open again and there was an entire pack of reporters and camera crews waiting inside, including Polly Horton.

Jenna was polite with them, but she explained quite simply that she couldn't comment on details that might compromise the meeting that she and Sam were about to have with Thorsborne. She did however introduce Sam as the representative of the distressed farmers of Wirralong.

'So, Sam,' Polly called out. 'Are you David about to do battle with Goliath?'

Sam knew she was deliberately teasing and for a moment he almost played up to her, adopting a pose similar to Michelangelo's famous naked statue of David, but Jenna had set the tone, so he simply shrugged and smiled.

'Wish me luck,' he said, smiling again, and he left it at that.

Afterwards, when Sam looked back on the day's proceedings, the actual meeting with Thorsborne was something of a blur. He hadn't known what to expect, but on their arrival they'd been confronted by a table with six stern-faced men and women, including the head honcho from Thorsborne's office in Geneva. Seated behind these were at least another six people, presumably lawyers or local mining managers, who occasionally leaned forward to pass sheets of paper or to whisper in an ear.

Jenna was asked to present her case and Sam could certainly remember the brick that lodged in his throat as she stepped up, lifting her chin, straightening her back and looking these blank-faced board members straight in the eye. Her voice was strong and confident and, skilfully, she seemed to address each of her targets personally.

To Sam, she was brilliant, and it was clear she had an immediate impact on her audience. While she was making an important point, someone from the back ranks tried to pass a note forward, and the Geneva chairman blocked him with a dismissive wave of his hand. The chairman's full attention was on Jenna.

Sam couldn't blame the guy, of course, and he wasn't surprised when this imposing chairman called a halt to the discussion before Jenna was even halfway through her list of recent payouts for successful class actions in Australia. She'd only had to mention amounts ranging up to four hundred million to convince the board that a settlement out of court was their best option—especially when she stressed that all these farmers were asking for was access to their river water.

In the end, it was Thorsborne's Australian manager who

was red-faced, as he tried to justify 'this most unfortunate oversight that must be quickly rectified'.

'We're an innovative company committed to world's best practice,' the manager protested. 'I'm sure we'll be able to look after our rights in the Wirralong region without depriving farmers of theirs.'

'Indeed,' the grey-haired Swiss mining magnate chimed in. 'As of today, I'm instructing your people on the ground here in Australia to make immediate arrangements for farmers to get their stock to water on our lease.'

By the time Jenna, Sam and the Thorsborne Chairman faced the media pack once again, there were smiles and handshakes all round.

AND, JUST LIKE that, it was over.

Jenna had made it look easy, but after weeks of tension, Sam was sure this moment should have felt bigger. Hell. Fenton was safe, and his cattle could once again drink from the river. The farmers of Wirralong no longer needed to break the law or to carry water tanks on the backs of trucks out to far-flung paddocks.

He supposed the euphoria would hit him when he reached home and he could share the good news with the folk of Wirralong. There'd be celebrations, for sure. Country style.

But now?

'You were brilliant,' he told Jenna. 'They didn't stand a chance.'

She looked a little flushed. 'I'm glad I was able to help.'

'On behalf of everyone at Wirralong—' He held out his hand. 'We're very grateful.'

It was crazy, as he shook her hand, to be remembering intimate details of their fling weekend.

Sam would have liked to mention Jenna's father—to suggest that he would have been proud of Jenna today—but he didn't want to embarrass her, or to make her cry. As another lump swelled in his throat, he looked out through the huge glass doors to the city street.

It was chock-a-block with traffic, and the footpaths were crowded with men and women of all ages, dressed alike in dark, sombre suits, all of them hurrying and unsmiling, while above the street, skyscrapers towered. The sight was enough to make him claustrophobic.

As he loosened his collar and tie, he thought, desperately, that there must be a trendy restaurant somewhere. Somewhere quiet with great food and good wine.

'We should be celebrating,' he told Jenna.

Chapter Seventeen

CELEBRATING?

A shiver skittered down Jenna's spine.

She knew Sam was right. Today's victory was a triumph on so many levels—an obvious success for him and for the other graziers of Wirralong, but a personal victory for herself as well.

A victory for the ten-year-old girl who'd walked into an outback shed to a scene of unbearable horror.

Sure, she'd taken on this case for Sam and his fellow farmers, but she knew, deep down, she'd also been doing this for her dad. And while this success could never make up for the tragedy of her father's death, Jenna was hoping that she might, at least, sleep a little easier now that she'd braved the outback and had this successful case behind her.

Sam was right, though. After many similar victories, a celebration with her client would be quite appropriate. But how could she celebrate with the one man she was hoping to forget?

She'd spent weeks trying to work Sam Twist out of her system, putting in longer hours than ever at the office, jogging more and more kilometres, devoting extra time at the gym. Without even consciously trying to lose weight, she'd gone down a whole dress size.

'Come on,' Sam urged her now, with that same sexy smile that had caught her off guard on the first night they'd met. 'Let me buy you lunch.'

'Will you be driving back to Wirralong afterwards?'

He was still smiling, but his gaze narrowed. 'Is that relevant?'

Jenna swallowed. 'I don't suppose so.'

But Sam was too shrewd. 'You're worried I'll want to stay overnight.' She could almost detect a teasing note now.

He was right, though. Of course she was worried that their lunch would be leisurely and delightfully drawn out, with the option of a hotel room at some point. Worried because it exposed her secret longings. Impossible longings she'd been working hard to suppress, despite the ludicrous number of times she'd sat alone in her apartment, replaying the TV segment of her and Sam on the riverbank.

She should remember, though, that today's outcome was a big deal for Sam. He'd never acted like he was stressed, but she knew he'd been living through long months of worry. Today's result couldn't lift the drought, but it was definitely worthy of a small celebration.

'Lunch would be great,' she said. 'I know the perfect place. I'll just ring and see if I can grab a spare table.' A minute later, she gave Sam the thumbs-up.

'Lead the way.' His smile was gorgeous and seared straight to her soul.

And the buzzing started again as they set off, weaving their way through the crush of pedestrians. The buzzing, plus a crazy, happy humming.

Jenna told herself she deserved a little happiness, too. She would take Sam to Luigi's. He'd love it. Atmosphere in spades, great food, amazing wines, brilliant rooftop views. For one afternoon, they could recapture a little of the magic they'd known for those brief few days in Wirralong.

As they stepped onto a busy pedestrian crossing with a crowd of others, she caught Sam's eye, saw the same sparkle that had almost stopped her in her tracks when she'd arrived at Cate and Craig's wedding, and now she almost skipped out of sheer happiness. For the rest of the day, she wouldn't listen to common sense. She just wanted to enjoy a final afternoon with this wonderful guy.

SAM HAD NO idea what to expect as the lift doors slid open. They'd arrived at the top floor of another skyscraper and when they stepped out into the corridor, the entrance to a restaurant was directly opposite. A rough stone wall was covered with a climbing jungle of plants. In the midst of them was the name Luigi's in stainless steel lettering. Through a window in the wall, he could see busy waiters and a glimpse of a spectacular cityscape view beyond.

Jenna looked excited. She clearly loved this place and Sam was sure he'd love it, too, although he'd probably have been happy in a greasy hamburger joint if Jenna had chosen it. He wasn't sure if another hour or two could change anything about their future, but he was about to give it his best shot.

They were greeted at the door by a ridiculously handsome Italian man, who seemed to know Jenna personally, and Sam tried not to wonder how many other guys she'd brought here. The interior was spacious and, although each table seemed to be occupied, the sound level was muted. Glass walls showed a breathtaking eagle's-eye view of the city below.

A waiter sailed past bearing huge white plates. Sam caught the aroma of Italian herbs and his stomach rumbled. He remembered that he hadn't eaten today and was instantly ravenous.

'This is great. Just what I needed,' he told Jenna and she flashed him a happy smile that made him feel he could leap tall buildings in a single bound.

'Jenna!'

They were halfway across the restaurant, escorted by a young waiter, when a stocky blond fellow in an expensive suit waved from a nearby table. A moment later the fellow was on his feet, hurrying toward them.

'Congratulations,' he cried, grinning broadly as he

slapped a hand on Jenna's shoulder. 'We've just heard the good news about the Thorsborne case.'

'Yes,' Jenna said. 'It went well.' After a quick apology to the waiter, she turned to Sam and it was hard to tell if she was happy about this intrusion. Introductions were necessary. The guy was Nigel Rowbotham, a fellow lawyer, who worked for the same firm as Jenna.

'Great to meet you,' Nigel said as he pumped Sam's hand.

Sam was happy enough to meet him, but he was also keen to be dining alone with Jenna.

'Geoff and Tony are here as well,' Nigel Rowbotham enthused, pointing to the table he'd vacated.

Two other men, equally well-groomed and expensively suited, smiled and waved, and Jenna waved back to them. Sam wasn't moved to add his smile to the mix.

So this, he assumed, was the exclusive boys' club, the band of lawyerly brothers Jenna had worked so hard to impress.

'Listen,' Nigel said. 'There's room at our table. Why don't you two join us? We've only ordered our wine so far. Come on. Tony's celebrating a win, too, and he's lashed out on a bottle of Grange.'

Bloody hell. Sam choked back his surprise. Grange Hermitage was Australia's most expensive wine. Seven hundred dollars a bottle. So much for the long, arduous hours city lawyers supposedly worked. Seemed they played hard, too.

Jenna was looking embarrassed. 'Gosh, no,' she said. 'We couldn't drink Tony's Grange.'

'Course you can. I'll order a bottle, too. It's Friday after all and you've got to celebrate.' Nigel turned to the waiter. 'You can seat two extras at our table, can't you?'

'Certainly, sir.' The young fellow gave a polite nod.

Sam needed to thump someone. The last thing he wanted was to share his lunch date with Jenna and a bunch of lawyers, no matter how successful, prestigious, or generous they might be.

Jenna was looking as frantic as he felt. 'Thank you, Nigel,' she said. 'But there are things I need to discuss with—'

The fellow waved this aside. 'Leave business till later. You two need to celebrate.'

Alone, Sam wanted to add. Problem was, these colleagues of Jenna's had been generous enough to encourage her to work on the Thorsborne case pro bono. They may have even helped her for all Sam knew and now they were being extra magnanimous.

Jenna must have been hit by similar misgivings. She'd been so strong during the meeting with Thorsborne, but now she was looking rather helpless and Sam supposed she was also concerned about making a fuss over dining alone with him. To do so would signal a personal interest in her client, and that was probably the last message she wanted to send to her colleagues.

Or to me, Sam reminded himself.

Even so, his impulse was to override the lot of them. This lunch was his idea. He'd planned to host Jenna, not the other way around, and he was a guy who liked to stick to his plans. But already two chairs had been added at the lawyers' table and the waiter was busy setting extra cutlery.

It was pretty damn clear that Sam was going to lose this battle. If he intervened now, there'd be huge embarrassment all round. Hardly the right scenario for a last-ditch attempt to win Jenna's heart.

More to the point, Jenna had worked hard to achieve respect and acceptance from her male colleagues, and it would be bloody mean-spirited to demand that he keep her to himself when this could well be a crucial opportunity to boost her career.

'I'm really sorry,' she whispered and she looked genuine-ly regretful, which was sweet of her, but it did little to cheer Sam.

He was on his best behaviour, however, as they joined her fellow lawyers, accepting their hearty congrats, along with shining glasses of Grange, while holding his end of their witty and urbane conversation.

The vibes from the lawyers weren't condescending, which was just as well, and Sam was pleased to sense their true regard for Jenna. Which was brilliant. There was even passing mention of a possible partnership in the firm for her, which he knew was the Holy Grail for all lawyers.

So, with a sinking heart, Sam managed to smile and to

keep up a smooth line of chat, but he reluctantly put the brakes on his dreams of seduction. Somehow in the past few weeks, a crazy miracle had happened and he'd discovered his perfect woman.

Now it was time to accept the painful truth. Jenna Matthews was a bloody good lawyer and this was where she belonged, amidst the skyscrapers and office blocks of a bustling metropolis.

For Sam, the end of this lunch would signal the time to retreat, to bid Jenna a gentlemanly farewell and to return to Wirralong, eternally grateful. Forever regretful.

Chapter Eighteen

*H*OW DID PEOPLE *get over the biggest mistakes of their lives?*

For weeks, Jenna had been asking herself this question without arriving at any kind of answer. It didn't help that her working life was all about avoiding mistakes wherever possible. As a corporate lawyer, she counselled clients on a daily basis, helping them with their business transactions, negotiating their contracts, reviewing their agreements, their mergers and acquisitions. But while these matters were sometimes complex, they seemed incredibly straightforward compared with interpersonal problems.

Jenna was beginning to wish she'd taken up family law. At least it might have given her a handle on how to get over a breakup.

Of course, the aftermath of a fling hardly warranted the term breakup, but that was the crazy thing. Saying goodbye to Sam had felt like the end of so much more than a simple fling.

It had felt truly momentous.

She told herself this was because she'd become involved

in the fence business with him, but when she lay awake at night, it wasn't the fence she was remembering. It was riding in a dusty ute with Sam. Getting up with him at one in the morning to feed orphaned lambs. Falling into bed with him again and making up silly poetry. Laughing with him. Making love with him. Crying her heart out in his arms.

If she'd been honest, she would have admitted right from that first weekend that there was something deep going on between them, but she hadn't once trusted her instincts and instead she'd held Sam at arm's length.

Now, she was left with the questions that had tortured her for weeks ... Why hadn't she confronted Sam with a few pertinent questions before she'd let him go? Why hadn't she at least *hinted* at the depth of her own feelings?

Unfortunately, the answers—pointing to a combination of cowardice and foolishness—weren't very palatable.

A MONTH AFTER the class action Jenna moved into her new office. It wasn't quite a corner office, but the next-best thing, with a massive oak desk and fabulous floor-to-ceiling windows offering impressive views across parkland and cityscapes.

She arrived early, planning to lug the last of her mountain of boxes into the new space before the working day officially began. But she couldn't resist taking a quick peek at her new favourite Facebook site—the Wirralong Community page.

And that was how she first learned about the rain.

At last. Rain in Wirralong. *Oh, my God.*

Someone had posted a map from the Bureau of Meteorology showing a massive, multi-coloured blob that stretched from the South Australian border right across to northeastern Victoria. Beneath the post were tons of 'likes' and smiley emoticons from happy Wirralong folk. And further down the page were wonderful pictures of rain-drenched streets, of swelling rivers and spreading puddles in paddocks. There was even a video of people dancing in the rain.

At the thought of Fenton's blistering paddocks being drenched at last, joy bubbled through Jenna like a geyser. She couldn't remember the last time she'd felt so happy or excited.

Desperate to know more, she checked a weather site and soon learned there was plenty more rain on the way. A week's worth of rain. Good rain. Drought-breaking.

At last the rivers and dams of the entire district would be full, the pastures would grow green again. The sheep and cattle would thrive and struggling farmers would breathe a sigh of relief. The pressure was off. They could take a step back from the brink of despair.

It was such wonderful news for Sam, for Cate and Craig, for Ted Jeffries, for all the worried people who'd filled the Wirralong hall to protest about the fence. Jenna was truly happy for them, so it made absolutely no sense that tears were streaming down her face. Worse, when she looked around at her spacious new office with its windows and desk, with its plush carpet and walls of built-in cupboards, she had never felt so spectacularly—so totally, no doubt about it—in the wrong place!

Abandoning the towering document boxes, she grabbed a box of tissues and her shoulder bag, and without bothering to blot her tears, she hurried outside. Sophie, her PA, had just arrived and was about to take her usual seat at her desk. When she saw Jenna, however, her face was an instant picture of worried dismay. 'What's the matter?' she cried, hurrying forward. 'Jenna, what's happened?'

Jenna gave her a soppy grin. 'It's raining in Wirralong.'

Sophie's eyes widened to saucers as she tried to compute this. 'Excuse me?'

Jenna was too impatient to explain properly. 'Wirralong,' she repeated. 'The drought's broken. Cancel all my appointments.'

'But—'

Jenna didn't wait for Sophie's 'buts.' She didn't want to hear them. Something more important had happened that she couldn't ignore.

IT WAS LATE morning by the time she arrived at Fenton with

her little car's windscreen wipers thrashing madly. Already the tracks leading into the property were slick with mud, but luckily her car's tyres hadn't slipped or bogged.

Throughout the journey she'd been making plans and giving herself pep talks. Building hopes and dreams. Now, as she pulled up in front of Sam's homestead, she was suddenly terrified. Should she have warned Sam she was coming? Would he be happy to see her? Or would he send her packing?

For all she knew, he might already have a new girlfriend.

It was only as she turned off the motor that she realised she'd left in such a rush that she hadn't even brought an umbrella. By the time she made it to Sam's front door, she'd resemble a drowned rat, which was hardly the best look for the romantic reunion she longed for. But she couldn't stay in the car all day.

Oh, well, here goes ...

Of course, she was drenched as soon as she opened the car door. The rain was cold and her grey silk blouse was instantly soaked, her hair plastered to her head.

I'm crazy. Sam will think I'm nuts.

But even before she set off through the sheeting downpour, she saw a figure hurrying across the verandah and down the front steps. Tall and masculine. There could be no doubt.

Sam.

He hadn't bothered with an umbrella or coat either and

already, as he closed the gap between them, his cotton shirt was soaked and was clinging to his chest, defining the magnificent shoulders and muscles that Jenna had recalled countless times in the past lonely weeks.

Now, her heart stumbled as she saw his gorgeous, puzzled smile.

'Jenna, what are you doing here?'

'It's raining. I had to come and see it.'

He wasn't scowling at her, which was a good start. His smile broadened. 'It's amazing, isn't it?'

'Fantastic. I'm so happy for you.'

'But you're getting wet.'

'Who cares?' Feeling totally giddy and reckless now that Sam seemed pleased to see her, Jenna lifted her arms and danced a little jig. She was laughing and probably crying as well and no doubt her blouse was as transparent as Sam's shirt.

Almost immediately, Sam was reaching for her, taking one of her hands in his, and with his other hand at her waist, he waltzed her around the car and over the gravel drive for the craziest most joyous dance of Jenna's life.

She was breathless by the time they came to a halt. Breathless and soaked from head to toe and, possibly, shivering.

'You know you're crazy,' Sam said, drawing her closer.

'Yes,' she said. 'I'm afraid I am.'

'I love crazy,' he said next and in the streaming rain he

hauled her hard against him and then they were kissing, hungrily, desperately, making up for lost time. They might never have stopped if Sam hadn't suggested that they should probably get out of their wet clothes.

Which was the best idea Jenna had heard in weeks.

They stripped off on the verandah, leaving their clothes in a sodden heap before they dashed inside. Sam quickly found fluffy towels and rubbed Jenna dry, kissing her repeatedly as he did so and Jenna knew there were important conversations to be had, but with the speed of her happiest fantasies, she found herself in Sam's bedroom, tumbling into his big, warm bed, pulling the doona over them both. Falling into bliss.

SOMETIME LATER, DRESSED in tracksuits and curled on the sofa in front of a cheerful fire, they talked as they sipped mugs of delicious hot coffee.

'At least we have one thing sorted,' Sam said.

'We're damn good in bed?' Jenna suggested.

He slid her a grin. 'Gold medal.'

'What are we going to do about it?'

'It's obvious we need to see each other way more often.'

Jenna nodded and she might have been blushing. She certainly felt hot and bothered again. She was desperate to tell Sam how she really felt, how much he'd come to mean to her.

'The problem is,' he said next, 'I'd really like to see you more than every few weeks. I don't suppose I could set up my swag in your office and camp there for the rest of our lives?'

Jenna's heart bounded. She shot him a quick searching glance. 'But you don't do commitment.'

'I *didn't* do commitment,' Sam corrected. 'That's true. Or at least it used to be true before—' The sparkle in his eyes might have held a glimmer of something else, a sudden vulnerability that made Jenna's breath catch. 'Before I met you,' he said next.

It was suddenly very important to set her mug aside. Having done so, Jenna turned to Sam, offering a shy smile.

'Well, I also have a confession to make,' she said. 'I—I—' Suddenly nervous, she had to swallow to ease her dry throat. 'I seem to have fallen in love with you.'

'Oh, Jen.' Sam's voice was low and rough, as he also abandoned his coffee and hauled her back into his arms. 'I love you so, so much.'

More kisses were needed—the very happiest, most fervent of kisses.

'I've missed you so much,' Sam said. 'I've been miserable and I haven't slept properly for weeks. I've been cranky as hell.'

'And I've missed you.'

'I love you,' Sam said again. 'You're so beautiful and

clever and brave and the whole time you're away, I can't stop thinking about you. I need you, Jenna.'

She snuggled closer. 'They're all the very reasons that I love you.'

Sam kissed her again and Jenna had never felt so full to bursting with happiness. Absolute, infinite, full-to-the-brim happiness.

'So many times I nearly drove to Melbourne and stormed your office,' he said as he released her.

'I think I might have liked my office being stormed.'

His happy smile dimmed a little. 'It's a problem though, isn't it?'

'My work?'

'Your work. My work. For both of us, our jobs are more than work. They're careers, a passion, a lifestyle.'

She nodded. 'I've been made a junior partner.'

'Wow.' Sam's smile was more complicated now. 'That's fantastic. Such a coup.'

'It is, yes.'

'I guess that's the answer then.' A new note of quiet determination in his voice was almost scary.

'How do you mean?' Jenna asked.

'You're needed in Melbourne. Trying to live together will be a major problem.' With a wry smile he shrugged. 'Unless I settle for the swag in your office option.'

'Or unless I set up here,' Jenna suggested boldly.

Sam blinked. 'Could you do that?'

'Reckon I could. I've given it quite a bit of thought. I've worked from Wirralong before, so I figure I can work from Fenton.'

His eyes were alight with hope now, a flash of the old Sam.

'You have a good phone line,' Jenna continued. 'You have Wi-Fi. And I wouldn't be the first lawyer to work out of town.' She offered him a reassuring grin. 'I've got it all worked out, you see. If you could spare a room, I could set up an office for teleconferencing.'

In her more fanciful moments over the past lonely weeks, she'd imagined this scenario in vivid detail.

'I can spare you as many rooms as you like,' said Sam. 'I can build you an entire new office. Whatever.'

'And I could start up a new arm of our firm that specialises in rural issues.'

'Jen,' Sam said softly. 'That's brilliant.'

They smiled at each other. The face-splitting, soppy smiles of lovers who knew they were meant for each other.

'And now,' she said, taking his big hand in hers. 'I need a progress report on my lambs.'

Epilogue

'SO, WHAT DO you think?'

As Jenna stood before the mirror in Wirralong's bridal shop, she had doubts about the white dress she'd just donned. The skirt was a little too lacy and frothy for her taste, but the strapless bodice fitted nicely and Cate, as well as Ivy, the store's owner, had been dead keen for her to try it on.

'I love it,' Ivy announced. 'I think it's perfect.'

'You look beautiful,' added Cate, who was to be Jenna's matron of honour and was pretending to be concerned that her pregnant tummy might show by the time of the wedding, although Jenna was pretty certain Cate was secretly hoping to show off her cute new bump.

Accepting their praise, Jenna studied her reflection again, picturing the wedding that she and Sam had planned. It was to be held at Wirra Station, which was not only a beautiful local venue, but would provide luxury accommodation for her city colleagues and their partners, all of whom were super eager to attend.

She pictured her Sam, dressed to the nines in his bridegroom's suit, and waiting for her—an echo of the day they'd first met. On her own wedding day, she hoped to see that same flash of appreciation in Sam's eyes that had robbed her of breath at that very first sighting. It was important to find the right dress.

Was this the one? Jenna gave a little twirl, so she could see the back and the way the skirt rustled when she moved.

'I'm not sure,' she said, but at that same moment, she caught a glimpse of a familiar figure staring through the shop's window.

Sam, who was supposed to be having some kind of business discussion with a stock and station agent, was on the footpath outside, watching her. Framed by two bridal mannequins, complete with veils and bouquets, he grinned at her and waved.

Jenna couldn't resist waving back.

'Oh, for heaven's sake!' Cate cried from behind her. 'Are you two crazy? Jenna, stop it! You've got to hide. You can't let Sam see you in your wedding dress.'

'But I don't think I'll be—'

'Hide!' Cate cried again, giving Jenna an anxious shove towards a change cubicle just as Sam strode through the shop's doorway.

Ivy looked startled and Jenna obediently ducked into the hiding space, but not before she caught another glimpse of her man, looking far too tall and broad shouldered and male, surrounded by the salon's rows of white frothy gowns.

Next moment, Cate yanked the curtain across, blocking Jenna's view.

'You can't come in here, Sam,' Jenna heard Cate order him. 'You've got to go. It's bad luck.'

'Bad luck?' Sam repeated, sounding puzzled.

Jenna poked her head around the curtain. In this ultra-feminine scene, filled with gilt mirrors and huge vases of white roses, her handsome fiancé looked totally out of place and all kinds of gorgeous in his blue checked shirt and chinos and leather riding boots.

'It's supposed to be bad luck if you see your bride-to-be in her wedding dress,' she explained.

'I only saw a flash of white,' offered Sam, who was looking highly amused by all the fuss and drama.

'You can always choose another dress,' Ivy suggested helpfully.

That was Jenna's plan. She'd already slid the zipper down and now she carefully stepped out of the dress.

Reaching around the curtain, she held it out to Ivy. 'Thanks, I will try a few more.'

'Of course.'

Then, hauling her cotton shift back on, Jenna hurried out barefoot to Sam. 'You're not supposed to be in here,' she told him.

'Yeah, I'm getting that message.'

'But I'm glad you came,' she added, rising on tiptoes to kiss him. And then, quietly, just for him, 'I'm not superstitious.'

'I know,' Sam murmured back and while their onlookers gave happy sighs, he wrapped his arms around Jenna and murmured close to her ear. 'What we have will last forever and that's more important than luck.'

Just the same, he departed quickly, and five minutes later, Jenna found her perfect dress.

Cate and Ivy were ecstatic, Jenna was overjoyed, and it was arranged that the dress could remain safely at the shop until the big day.

I MUSTN'T CRY ...

Jenna couldn't believe how emotional she felt as she arrived at Wirra Station. Everything was perfect. The smooth lawns were bright green after a good season of rain. Her city friends and the wonderful new friends she'd made since moving to Wirralong were all ready and waiting in rows of seats decorated with white ribbons.

Her sister, Sally, and her best friend, Cate, looked beautiful in their floating bridesmaids' gowns of softest blush pink. And her mum and Sam's mum looked utterly elegant and dignified in their beautiful outfits of grey lace and cranberry silk, respectively.

Sal's husband Tom was giving Jenna away, and she did think of her dad, wishing he could be there, too. But he'd left her a legacy, an important lesson about courage.

And she remembered that lesson now, as the sun spread a rose-gold smile across the sky and she saw Sam standing tall, ready and waiting, for her. No, she wouldn't cry today. Her eyes were on the future. Their future.

She sent him a smile and when he smiled back, she saw a flash in his eyes, a flash of love and deep promise, and her heart was aglow as she set off to meet him.

The End

The Outback Brides of Wirralong

Book 1: *Lacey* by Fiona McArthur

Book 2: *Tess* by Victoria Purman

Book 3: *Jenna* by Barbara Hannay

Book 4: *Emma* by Kelly Hunter

Available now at your favorite online retailer!

Don't miss the first Outback Bride Series

Book 1: *Maggie's Run* by Kelly Hunter

Book 2: *Belle's Secret* by Victoria Purman

Book 3: *Elsa's Stand* by Cathryn Hein

Book 4: *Holly's Heart* by Fiona McArthur

Available now at your favorite online retailer!

About the Author

Barbara Hannay is a former high school English teacher who was first published in 1999. Since then she has written over forty books for Harlequin and has published eight single title novels with Penguin Australia.

With more than twelve millions copies sold worldwide, Barbara's novels have earned her five RITA nominations from Romance Writers of America and she won a RITA award in 2007. She is also the recipient of two Romantic Book of the Year awards in Australia and one of her novels is currently being developed as a television movie by Brainpower in Canada. Barbara lives with her writer husband on a misty hillside in Far North Queensland.

Thank you for reading

Jenna

If you enjoyed this book, you can find more from all our great authors at TulePublishing.com, or from your favorite online retailer.

TULE
PUBLISHING

CPSIA information can be obtained
at www.ICGtesting.com
Printed in the USA
LVHW110751190820
663527LV00017B/1172